By-Catch

A Shamus Pickford Story

By

David Earth

David Earth's other titles:

Turtle Bay
A Trip to the Myakka Cutoff
Riviera Marina!

This is a work of fiction. All the characters and events portrayed in this book are fictional, and any resemblance to real people or actions is purely coincidental.

Author's Note

The Shamus Pickford stories are all rooted in Southwest Florida, where I aim to inject culture, the working man/woman struggles, the hardships, and the underbellies of everyday Floridians into my work. At times, I feel I've done them justice.

Florida's rapid growth has made it increasingly difficult for the simple-living waterman to sustain his way of life. That's one of the reasons I felt compelled to write these stories—to preserve in amber the "way it was," as vital to our cultural memory as plankton is to an oyster. With so much of Florida's past being swallowed up and paved over, the responsibility of remembering what once was now falls to longtime locals and storytellers.

These stories were written in the quiet hours—on days off, in stolen moments of spare time. The locations described throughout these books, and in most of my salt-soaked work, are real places, or at least, they were when the stories first took shape. As I write this, some of those very spots stand on the brink of erasure, threatened by the steady march of development. Bearing witness to this transformation provides a constant, if bittersweet, source of inspiration.

Year after year people flock to Florida, in specifics the Southwest coast, where it's dodged the dozers longer than the east coast. But as of late, it seems Pandora's box has finally been open. Huge corporations have, over time, weaseled their way into the community, funded many different programs to the unwitting recipients, only to come collect in the way of environmental destruction.

This note is by no means a call to protest. Growth is a force that cannot be stopped but must be done with the environment a top concern.

The short Shamus Pickford books can be on the technical side, some confusing lingo, or mentions of a strange location, that may only be familiar to the locals, who have lived in the areas described. It was not intentionally written that way.

Getting these stories "out there" has been an arduous process with many setbacks. It's hard to say whether I'd continue these past three or four.

The first blip of Shamus Pickford and his associates came to me when a friend and I were casting lures at a dock in a private basin on the east coast of Charlotte Harbor in the early 2000s (nearly 20 years before its first publication). I came to understand it from the bow of my skiff, watching the land flatten beneath the teeth of machines, as hulking new structures rise faster than the eye could blink. The basin described in these pages is real—still there, still fished, still breathing—but like so much of old Florida, its days may be numbered. The model for Shamus's house with the boat ramp was there at one point, only to have been torn down, and in its place a monstrosity of a house built overtop the ruins. Growth is growth.

It was sad to see it go, and I tried to remember it the best I could. I'd spent a lot of time fishing in that basin and along those docks, that I felt the need to preserve its memory, or at least a vague motif.

These books are not perfect. They aren't massive works of literature either, but I hope they capture interest, if only for a moment. When it was time to sit down and finally hash these things out, I did a good portion out on my skiff. The rough drafts lived nomadically in my head for years and prying them out clearly, and onto paper, was no easy task.

They were written mostly outdoors, which is where I choose to write the majority of my stories—it's where the muse is the strongest. Outdoors can be extremely inspirational. For me, a fine view and a cup of coffee is motivation at its best. I've had an on-again off-again relationship with this series over many years before struggling to their final drafts. I honestly thought I'd never finish them, but here we are.

"Man is the only varmint that sets his own trap,
baits it, then steps in it."
--John Steinbeck

"A golden rule of angling philosophy is not to
interfere with any fisherman's peculiar ways of
being happy, unless you want to be hated."
--Zane Grey (Tales of Fishes)

"I think there is some kind of divine order in the universe. Every leaf on every tree is unique. As far as we can see, there are other galaxies, all slowly spinning, numerous as the leaves in the forest. In an infinite of planets, there has to be an infinite number with lifeforms on them. Maybe this planet is one of the discarded mistakes. Maybe it's one of the victories. We'll never know."

--Travis McGee

By-Catch

Chapter One

From my captain's chair, I watched Sara Albright at the bow of my skiff, standing nervously as she scanned the water for any sea monsters she imagined lurking below. I'd assured my mid-twenties admirer that the danger was minimal, but she needed to see for herself. Her heightened caution was justifiable, given that her sole weaponry consisted of only a calf-strapped dive knife and a sketched-out mindset—so I didn't push. As an act of bravery, she dove boldly into the warm, sun-spangled waters of Charlotte Harbor and surfaced. Sara initially swam with caution, but she soon settled, swam near the edge of the gunwale, and retrieved my Hawaiian sling. I noticed her messing with it.

"Remember," I said, demonstrating with my hand. "Just hold the spear and draw back the rubber band, then let it rip."

"Got it," she said.

"Also, if you spear anything, please, make sure it's legal, okay? And remember," I brought up my arms, spread my hands a foot apart, "snapper gotta be ten inches. Fork to tail."

"Kinda hard to tell from in the water," she said, spitting out a stream of saltwater.

"Do your best."

"Always do." Sara swam off wearing nothing but bikini bottoms, the knife, a snorkel, and a pair of dive fins.

I cracked a beer, stretched in my captain's chair, and grinned while Sara's head was half-submerged, searching the water underneath. And then she dove. In truth, Sara was the embodiment of every youthful dream I'd ever had, every reckless fantasy come to life.

I heard a puff of air though a snorkel. Sara had resurfaced.

"Shamus!" Sara said, swimming to the boat, the rubber band looped around her ankle.

I rose and noticed her towing the Hawaiian sling, dragging a tail-speared mangrove snapper behind her. She began treading water with one hand and then held up the snapper in the other.

"This one look legal?"

"It sure as hell does," I said, kneeling. "How big do you think it is?"

"Not sure—biggun' though." She flipped the sling, and the fish into the boat.

The snapper was a fine specimen indeed, and even as its tail curled, it was well within the legal limits. Mangrove snapper thrived in a variety of marine environments—from easy-access canals and man-made offshore wrecks to shallow seagrass beds and windswept flats. Others lurked deep in the shadows of sunken wrecks, tucked far out of reach. A sought-after species, that for many nights, had satisfied my insatiable cravings for seafood.

I handled the fifteen-inch fish with respect, letting it lay at ease under my hand. After slipping it from the spear's tip and measuring it, I was wrong, the fish measured eighteen inches. I placed it inside the cooler gently under ice.

Sara swung a leg up in hopes of climbing aboard but only managed halfway before slipping back into the water after a high-shriek yelp. I giggled.

She raised her hand, swiping matted golden-brown hair from her eyes. "Can I get some help?" she said, arm raised, hand opened palmed.

I delayed long enough for her to cringe at the unknowns below. Sara was progressing toward overcoming her perennial fear of the water at an exponential rate.

"Sara," I said. "The fact is you cannot control the inevitable. If you're going to get bit or stung, you are going to get bit or stung. Over-cautiousness is a noble trait but will eventually lead to regret."

Her eyes rolled.

"I saw that." I said, and leaned in, snatched her hand firm yet gentle, boosted her above my head, and cupped her firm derriere. Her body slid down, pressing soft breasts against my chest. Her elfish ears pierced through her saturated blonde hair that dripped water between her chest and onto the skiff's deck. I found her eyes first. She smiled, exposing an upper row of professionally aligned teeth. We kissed.

After our mid-afternoon workout, Sara and I packed up the skiff and began the short trip back to the houseboat.

Following the incident involving my friends Eliot and Klinger, an emotional void developed in my life, one that only Sara could fill, a primal craving after a tragic event. We met at her house after I answered an online ad for a '95 Toyota pickup her dad had listed. Sara was out front, push-mowing the lawn beneath the heat. After some back-and-forth, I offered to trade my enclosed box trailer for the truck, and her father agreed. When he mentioned that Sara could use a side hustle, I left with more than a pickup—I'd gained a new employee. A few months later, that working arrangement quietly evolved into something more, although we hadn't yet discussed anything related to our relationship's trajectory.

Sara was currently helping out with my struggling side gig—scraping barnacles off the hulls of crusty boats. It wasn't a prolific business, and after a slow winter, my client list had become meager at best, which was okay with me, because I felt with charter fishing alone, I could sustain the lifestyle I desired. Unbeknownst to most, I operate illegitimately, without a license or rules. Yet, with the truth laid before them, not one client had ever turned away.

Back at the houseboat, anchored midway along Charlotte Harbor's West Wall, we cleaned up and I started lunch.

My custom twenty-four-foot houseboat was built above a pontoon frame, and the thin walls, poor steering, and a rotting plywood floor were its best features. It was a cozy rustic-style liveaboard, equipped with all the usual necessities—galley, couch, twin bed, and a broken head. It had taken countless sunlit days to bring it to its current state of seaworthiness—one hundred square feet of ongoing effort, drunken pride, and piece-together grit. And for its maiden voyage, I imagined no finer companion than Sara.

Power came from a beat-up ninety-horsepower engine with a flakey fuel pump. So I often hip-towed my skiff as a precaution—just in case the engine gave out and I needed a backup.

"Hey," Sara said. "We're not doing Panko again, are we?"

In a cast iron pan, I was warming up a cup of olive oil on the small camping stove. "What else would you prefer? It's all we've got."

Sara opened the cooler. "Oh, I don't know. We've got milk," she replied, lifting a carton of vitamin D.

I turned sharply. "Don't you even think about it—"

She swooped her hand, smacking me on the backside. "I'm just yoking your tiller."

I embraced her, brushed golden blonde hair behind her left ear and kissed her neck. She quivered, accepted the offer, and tilted her head stiff while my lips searched for the sweet spot.

"Hey," she said swarmed with lust. "You're going to burn lunch."

I came up for air. "Let it burn…"

She replied in a weak, fluttering voice, "I want to eat my monster mango, Shamus."

Still kissing her neck, "I'll give you a monster mango…"

I lifted and carried her to the twin-size bed under a box window, and we tangled like a steamed pretzel. Not long after, in the sauté pan, the olive oil began to crackle. I leaped up and rushed to the camping stove.

"Hey, where yah goin'?" She rolled out from the bed wrapped in a white sheet.

"I'm going to put the fish on," I said, checking the oil. "We need our strength."

Sara let the sheet slip from her hands, brushed past me, and disappeared through the side cabin door, skipping out onto the houseboat's bow.

"Hey, now where are you going?" I gazed through the bow windows, spellbound, and at that moment, utterly consumed by her beauty.

Sara decided to go for a swim before lunch. Bending over, long legs stretched below symmetrical butt dimples, she clapped her hands together, interlocked her fingers, lifted them above her head, and sprang a tan-lined body into the water.

I removed a stubborn cork from a bottle of wine and wondered how life could get any better. That's when the phone rang. It was my buddy, Cliff, who owns a local health food deli he called *Gribbles* in downtown Punta Gorda.

I answered, bordering on a shout. "Cliff?"

"Yeah, what's up?" I heard through the phone.

"Not much. Sitting on the West Wall, enjoying the houseboat." I was watching Sara climb a three-rung stainless-steel bow ladder onto the front deck. I added into the phone, "And the view is *amazing.*"

Sara was now drying off, shaking all her body parts.

I snapped from my trance. "So, what's going on, Cliff?"

"Not much … just been working. Hey, I wanted to see if you could help me with a catering job tonight?"

Through the large square windows, Sara strode to the cabin door.

"Tonight?" I said. "Um—not sure I can make it…"

Sara slipped through the door and made herself known. "Who's that?" she asked.

I glanced and whispered, "Cliff," and then returned the phone to my ear.

"Is that Sara?" Cliff asked.

I kicked her in the butt. "Yeah, she's helping me break in the ol' houseboat."

"Oh, yeah? You two been getting serious, huh?"

"Yeah, something to that nature. Going on several months now."

Sara retaliated by teasing to cover up.

"Gotcha," Cliff said. "Sorry, didn't know you had company. I'll call my dad and see if he wants to help."

I kept my eyes on Sara. "Hey, can Sara come along? She's great with food."

She shifted her hips, pouted up her lip, and then relaxed to a smile.

"Um … sure. I don't see why not," Cliff said—paused, and added, "I can't pay both of you, though."

"Don't worry about it." I winked at Sara. "We'll split it."

"Okay, sounds good, then. I'll text you the details later."

I hung up the phone.

"Good with food?" Sara said with a crinkled brow. "That's all you could say?"

"Yeah, that was sort of lame, huh?"

She shrugged it off, relaxed her shoulders, and swept the hair from a soft peak of collarbone. Then both of her thumbs pointed inward. "Uh-huh—well, you'd better get this while its hot if you want to have time to enjoy it."

****

A couple hours later, we puttered into my home port—a small, private basin tucked along the eastern shore of Charlotte Harbor, the place I proudly call my backyard. The vast, glassy water stretched out like polished aluminum foil, mirroring the cloudless sky above in perfect, shimmering stillness. On cue, the resident dolphin greeted us using its signature tail slap.

Last year was bad for Charlotte Harbor after a nasty red tide bloom, and my basin became packed with mullet, leaving an abundance of dolphin snacks. They say it was the mullet that convinced the dolphin to stay. I'd named it Spinner.

As I idled along, I came upon the property of my neighbor, Flip Pees. His house appeared eerily empty, and since Eliot Waldrup's funeral, he'd been away often. For thirty-five years he and Eliot had been the best of friends and together fished commercial mullet for three decades. Witnessing the death of a friend could unmoor even the soundest mind, sending a man down a road he never meant to travel. The events that unfolded at the old Turtle Bay fish shack last year caused sorrow in the lives of many people. My good friend Klinger and I were fishing in Turtle Bay's backcountry and saw an unexpected package drop from the fuselage of a small plane. After a poorly executed investigation, and at the end of the day, a fine man was dead and another bereaving.

****

Docking the ungainly beast of a houseboat with the skiff in tow was a tedious task, one that required more patience than finesse. On its first delivery, I'd drank one too many cocktails and piloted her into the crumbling seawall, denting one pontoon, so I wasn't too concerned about damage.

This time the dockage was decent, and after an acceptable mooring, I found the lone structurally sound cleat and lashed the skiff to it. Soon as we were tied and locked in, Sara sprinted toward the house.

"Hey, where you going?" I asked.

Her upper body spun around, producing swing to her hair, which crossed a round face, partially obstructing her brown eyes. "I'll be *right* back, jeez."

It didn't take a genius to figure out where she was going. The work in progress included the houseboat's head.

Now that the hulking houseboat was secure, I moseyed up to the house where I heard the soft spray of water. Sara was in the shower. I also detected my new pup Scupper was missing. Normally, she waited for me at the front door. Through the screen door, overlooking the disarray of tangled backyard debris, I peeked outside and called to her.

Scupper had become my new four-legged companion. For months I'd catch fleeting glimpses of her wandering the neighborhood. So, I decided to get smart, and after many bags of dog food, she allowed me close enough to scratch her belly. It was a groundbreaking establishment of trust, and over time, we've become great friends.

After I meandered the yard, panting broadcasted from an adjacent palmetto thicket. Scupper emerged leaping like a gazelle through the overgrown palmettos that surrounded the property. If mowed regularly, my property could have great curb appeal—I cared about no such things.

"Here, girl!" She followed me into the house wagging her tail.

Sara had draped a couple spaghetti-strapped tops and a pair of board shorts over the arm of the couch. "This is all I got."

I glanced over her selection. "Hmmm…"

"Well?"

I turned to her and smiled as she stood in a red bra. "I like what you're wearing right now."

Her cheeks dropped. "I'm serious, Shamus. What should I wear to the catering job?"

"Um—jeans and a T-shirt should be fine. Cliff will have aprons to wear."

"Aprons? We have to wear *aprons?*"

"Well, yes," I answered. "It is an important job, and the look really sells professionalism."

She found a split hair and brought it up to her eyes. "I'll need to go home and pick something out."

"Really?"

"Yes, I can't wear this," she said, and swept a hand across the front of her half-naked body.

I looked her up and down with an irresistible grin. "The apron should cover most of it."

"Whatever," she said, snagging the clothes and scooting into the bedroom.

Moments later, just as Sara prepared to leave, I received a text message from Cliff:

Meet at 22120 Palm Tree Drive, PGI at 6 p.m.

Dinner starts at 7 p.m.

Bring a couple bags of ice.

Thanks.

"Cliff?" Sara asked.

"Yeah, we need to be in Punta Gorda Iles at six o'clock."

"Six? It's already five o'clock now."

"I know. We need to hurry." I pressed my hand to her back. "Go home and change. I'll come by and pick you up on my way, cool?"

"I guess…" She became lost in her mind. "Maybe I'll just sit this one out. One hour is not enough time—"

I slipped behind, pulling her close, nestling my chin into the sweet spot between the shoulder and neck, and kissed. "I'd like it if you came. It'll be fun, I promise."

She leaned her head on mine. "I'll go … jeez."

"Perfect. You better get going."

Sara scratched Scupper behind the ears and out the door she went, climbing into a forest green Ford F-150. She started it, rolled down the windows, and upped the music. It didn't matter what song played on the radio, she sang along to it—an adoring unbridled happiness.

Now, in a pragmatic mull, on time for the catering job was highly unlikely.

Chapter Two

After picking up Sara and ice, we arrived at the catering job ten minutes late.

Cliff was unloading kitchen gear next to his catering box van. Cliff Fleming was a northern transplant, but after spending most of his twenty-nine years in Florida, more time than anywhere else, it just made sense to call it home. When people asked where he was from, he said Florida without hesitation. He was a multitasking master and constantly wore hats that covered a receding hairline. He was tall, half-bald, and the hardest worker I'd ever known.

"What's up?" he asked, poking his head out of the van.

"Not much. Sorry we're late."

"Ahh—it's cool, only a few minutes."

I stood rigid with hands on my hips. "Where do we start?"

"So, right now…" Cliff was removing folded tables from the van. "…just settin' up the food line." He handed me the tables. "Take these to the lanai."

I tucked the fold-out plastic table under an arm. "No problem."

"Oh, and Shamus?"

"Yeah?"

"Go around back."

"Will do," I said, then mumbled, "The riffraff always stays hidden and blends into the background." Admittedly, it was where I preferred to be anyway.

I grasped the other table, left Cliff and Sara, and went ahead to the back side of an enormous waterfront mansion. Fresh-cut St. Augustine crunched under my feet. The place seemed endless with its lush landscaping running in rows, where elegant coconut palms leaned, growing horizontally for a few years before finishing with upward-facing crowns. Through their long-feathered fronds, the pleasant drip of coconut bushels hung like grapes. Sky-scraping royal palms also lined in purposeful rows while professionally trimmed flowering viburnums boxed in the entire property, down to the hundred-plus feet of bright, white seawall.

Not long after, I came upon a two-thousand-square-foot lanai—twice the size of my entire house. At the center, a kidney-shaped pool, the focal point, was bordered by a perimeter light, a thoughtful feature that gave the drunks one last warning before they stumbled in.

We had set up in the far corner next to the sliding glass door that led into the kitchen, and after the arrival of the guests, and a thirty-minute prep, dinner was hot and ready to plate.

In the crowd, numerous old men, retired types, wearing loud Hawaiian shirts, began swaying to a generic reggae Ska-riff playing from the deco-rock molded speakers hidden amongst the wicker furniture. Mixtures of middle-aged women and men also milled throughout the gathering. A younger crowd had separated from the elders, tucking into a dark corner of the lanai into a tight-knit faction. The younger men shared one unmistakable trait: raccoon-like tan lines across their eyes—a clear testament to the countless hours they'd spent in the sun.

Alcohol was free at the open bar, and the laughing and giggling women, who stood close to their men, were beginning to loosen.

Sara stood to my left behind a tin container that kept warm garlic-seasoned steamed vegetables. Cliff stood beside her aligning rows of tin containers that encapsulated the steamed main course: filet and/or grouper. I was on salad detail.

Encouraging my eyes to wander, they came to rest on Sara's arched back, furtively slipping down, lured toward black, stretched-thin slacks which concealed a perfect frame. As I lost thoughts to the imagination, a man waddled to my station hitching up the rim of his pants over top an overhanging, fat-impregnated gut.

"Hello, sir," I greeted. "Salad?"

He ignored my greeting while in disgust and focused on the salad. He was a short, bald, beady-eyed man who had the longest set of curly black eyebrows I'd ever seen.

I dug in the serving spoon and lifted the fresh-cut romaine lettuce, croutons, and parmesan cheese. "Salad, sir?" I repeated.

He looked up in a serious gruff. "Where's the wine?"

My fake smile widened. "Right over there, sir." I pointed toward the open bar twenty feet away.

Sara smiled at me and whispered, "Good job."

As the night rolled on, the pool screen-enclosed lanai protected us from the mangroves, and the unremitting no-see-ums that attack within the Florida night. It was nearing summer and doing nothing but standing still, I began to sweat.

Toward dinner's end, two raccoon-eyed fellows strolled along, inspecting the buffet table where Cliff, Sara, and I had prepared dessert—a simple scoop of caramel-ladled vanilla or chocolate ice cream.

The two were confident in their movements, seemed to desire secrecy, careful that no one could hear them talking—especially the "nonexistent" caterers. I pretended to be invisible but turned an ear. Both men wore matching fishing shirts, tight jeans, and whose similar mirror-green reflective sunglasses sat atop their flat-billed hats. The smaller man had weight to him, hair dark, and sprouts of chest hair peeked between his shirt buttons. The other, blond, tall, wiry in an athletic sort of way, stood antsy. His face composed a stark readiness to let loose information, something important that only the intended target was to know. He would have made a terrible poker player—had tells all over the place. He paused and moved his eyes too much— dead giveaway. He then motioned to his compact, battleship-tough partner to look around for eavesdropping ears, and to be sure no one had the ability to even lip read.

The supposed tall, blond leader said with a spoiled, cocky smile, "Them pens are locked up good and tight."

The short guy turned his hat backwards and said from the corner of his mouth, "Did you put enough cut ladyfish inside?"

"Ready as a pregnant bull."

I leaned closer and heard, "Easy pickin's…"

"Redfish magic," the shorter one said with a mischievous grin.

I wasn't sure what all that meant, but it didn't sound respectable.

Cliff strode near, handing me plastic plates. "Take these; pass 'em out."

I breezed past the two men as though I were invisible, making brief eye contact with the suspected leader. He moved his hand to his buddies' shoulder, gave me a halfhearted smile, and turned him closer.

As I handed out the dessert plates to the remaining guests, I couldn't help but overhear copious chatter about the start of the big redfish tournament taking place this weekend.

I wasn't fishing tournaments these days, but back when I was a greenhorn charter captain, hungry for every dollar I could haul in, I'd guided a handful of deep-pocket clients I couldn't afford to turn away. Over time though, I grew to loathe the competition, especially after witnessing all the pathetic, unsportsmanlike etiquette, and therefore renounced my participation. And not to mention, the tournaments were unpermitted and privately ran events that used state fisheries to bring a profit. And these fishing tournaments also bring in hundreds of non-local, big-balls flats boats with more horsepower than brains. Unlike me, they had no qualms about tearing through Charlotte Harbor's seagrass beds, even on a dead low tide.

It was somewhat a spectacle watching each boat launch on plane—one after another, shooting massive rooster tails. To me, protecting the fishery and the environment was my main concern. One reason I gravitated towards light-tackle guiding in the first place was so I could take out clients, and when they catch fish, educate them on the proper releasing techniques, which was to return the fish unharmed.

Back at the catering table, prior to cleaning up, Cliff and Sara were serving some of the last few guests.

Feeling somewhat cocky, I swooped to the open bar, snagged a cold beer, and cracked it open. I leaned against the round wooden lip, observant to the high-dollar mingling.

At the far side of the lanai, near the corner of the pool cage, the herd of younger guests remained congregated, forming their own private party. Plumes of cigarette smoke levitated through the night air as laughter carried in quick bursts across the pool. I gulped more beer and snuck back to the catering table and eased in next to Cliff.

"Hey, where's Sara?" I asked.

He nodded toward the kitchen sliding doors. "Bathroom."

"Gotcha," I said—leaned and whispered: "Hey, you know the redfish tournament's this weekend, right?"

Tying up a filled trash bag, he said, "Sure do."

"Yeah, that's what *I* heard."

Cliff finished the ties into a tight knot. "I always forget when those start."

"Yeah, me too." I glanced into the kitchen—didn't see Sara anywhere. "Hey, I'll be right back."

Cliff didn't look up and continued cleaning. "Okay, brother."

The sliding glass doors that lead into the kitchen were three times thicker than my home doors and weighed four hundred pounds apiece. As I opened the door, a cold burst of air smacked me in the face.

Through the brightly lit, stainless-steel-loaded, marble countertop kitchen, I came to a fork. One direction led to the foyer, and the other down a door-lined hallway. I assessed the immediate floor under the first door for occupancy, and the light was on. I tapped my knuckle.

"Ocupado," said the woman's voice behind it.

I pressed my ear to the door, and spoke in a Mid-Western twang, "Ma'am, your kind ain't allowed to use these facilities. They're for guests *only*. The help uses the portable blue toilet at the construction site next door... Um, ma'am?"

Through the door, I heard Sara's voice. "Excuse me?"

I paused, trying not to laugh, and added, "That's right, *ma'am*. This *here* is a *private* party."

"Who in the *hell* do you think you are?" she said and swung the door open. When she saw it was me, her hand smacked me in the chest before adjusting the apron. "Shamus, that's not funny."

I pressed her body, and mine, into the bathroom and closed the door. She was easy to lift, and I eased her into the sink's bowl, which was the right size for holding her. I raised my hand and tucked a lock of hair behind her ear, leaned in, but I knocked over a weaved basket. It hit the tile floor, and its contents scattered.

"Whoops," I said.

Her voice was silky. "Just leave it."

"Let me just pick it up quick, hang on…" I assured her with a kiss.

I left her for a moment melting into the sink and gathered the items. Toothbrush, dental floss, razor, and a bright red-capped prescription bottle. The prescription was for Graham Northwood, and it read: *Propranolol.*

I showed Sara.

She read the label, ignored it, and dunked it into the basket. "Forget it!" she said and pulled me back between her legs.

Minutes later, we slipped back to the buffet tables. Cliff had condensed the leftover food into a single serving, tin container. He swung the food tray to the counter behind him. "Have fun?"

"What do you mean?" I said, fixing my own apron, wearing a smile.

Sara and her red cheeks brushed by me carrying the trash bag I had tied earlier. She wasn't ready for publicity and headed toward the front of the house.

I turned, thumbing out toward the mingling, and said to Cliff, "Guess what I overheard one of these guys saying?"

"What's that?"

"I heard…" I paused, scoped the lanai, searching for the men in question. They were not in sight. "I heard two guys talking in private about 'Them pens are good.' And something about enough bait 'inside' and 'easy pickin's.'"

He raised a brow. "Them pens are good? What's that mean?"

"No clue. Any ideas?"

"Are those guys fishing the tourney?" he asked.

"They fit the bill."

"Then, I think you *know* what it means."

"What?" I said jokingly. "That they're going to trap redfish?"

"Either that…" he said—then peeked roundabout. "Or they've already *been* trapped."

I stuck a finger in my ear for effect. "What?"

He grinned. "I'm saying, maybe they've already fished the tournament … if you *know* what I mean…"

I understood Cliff's point. The notion that someone had stashed redfish in a holding pen to retrieve during a tournament was nothing short of a despicable, gutless trick that could stain the spirit of the sport.

My face began to swell with blood. "To cheat is what you're saying?"

"Pretty much." He shoved the food container into my chest. "Take this."

I whispered, "Those fish are my livelihood!"

"I hear you, brother." Cliff lifted an iced tea dispenser and started for the screen door.

I followed, taking deep breaths.

At a hose spigot attached to the side of the house, Cliff dumped the remaining tea into a towering potted Ginkgo.

I observed. "I didn't know trees like sweet tea."

"It's un-sweet," he corrected. "It's good for them. Something with the tannic acid. Makes 'em grow strong, like bull. You didn't know that?"

"Had never crossed my mind," I said, following him to driveway.

We reached his van, and he opened the rear doors, letting out the aroma of recently cooked meat.

"This leftover food up for grabs?" I hinted.

"I'll take some; probably donate some."

"These people don't want the leftovers?" I asked.

"Now, do these people look like they eat leftovers?"

"Good point. I'll take some, too."

I piled up grouper, salad, and one medium-rare steak.

In Sara's absence, I said, "I'm going to put this in my truck. Be right back."

Surf and Turf steam-fogged the warm plastic container. As I crossed the street and skipped along the front of the triple-lot house, members of the younger crowd were lingering in the driveway smoking cigarettes and holding bottled beers, figuring out their next stop for alcohol. One of them was Sara. She was speaking to the tall guy I had overheard. I stopped mid-stride across the street because of it and stared. She noticed me and broke away. I continued moving to my truck and placed the food on the driver's seat and closed—more like slammed—the door.

As soon as I spun around, she swept up. The only light was the streetlight illuminating her white cheeks. Her dark blonde hair remained partially tied up in a skilled bun. Loose strands had slipped their way through the tightly pinned hair sculpture and floated across her face. She sucked her cheeks in, as though impersonating a fish.

"Hey…" she said, oozing subliminal overtones, of which only an intimate lover was immune.

I nodded toward the group. "Who's that?"

"Who? Those guys? Oh, they're no one. They just wanted to compliment us on the food, is all."

I mumbled the reply, trying to hide my annoyance. "I know who they wanted to compliment…"

"What did you say, Shamus?" She gripped my hand, interlocking our fingers. "Why? Jealous?"

Her grip offered some comfort, but I still felt vacant. "*Nooo*, but they should thank Cliff. He did most of the work."

"Oh, they were just being nice." She smiled. "No *big deal.*"

It was an apology that I would accept whether I liked it or not.

Approaching Cliff's van, his organizational skills were on full display as the equipment had been loaded and neatly packed. At first sight, all that was missing were the serving tables, so Sara and I skedaddled along the flank of the house, to the side lanai, and stepped through the screen door. Cliff was speaking to an older gentleman. Sara and I approached.

"Shamus," Cliff said. "I want you to meet Graham Northwood. This is *his* party."

I shook his hand, one which felt like a bag of limp sausages, and then congratulated him on his enormous house.

"Oh, it took a lot of work to get her looking this way," he pointed out. "You know the Miss' is very particular on her ambiance."

"I bet."

He spoke to Sara. "Oh, and who's this lovely lady? I've been waiting to meet her all night."

Before I could introduce Sara as anything, she snuck out her hand. "I'm Sara," she said, and rolled her eyes toward me, added, "For now, I'm Shamus' girlfriend. We're both friends of Cliff's."

"Oh? Is that right?" The man eyed me.

He was a tall man, maybe six-foot-four and rail thin; had a small hunch in his back. No surprise; tall men were prone to spinal issues. He had a snowman's nose and cheekbone contours that sat puffed under his eyes. He was wearing a bright yellow, short-sleeved collared shirt above white pleated pants and tan sandals. When speaking, he projected a certain calmness, similar to those who have adjusted well to financial freedom. His voice was warm, inviting, trustworthy.

"What line of work are you in?" he asked. "Shamus, it is?"

Here we go, I thought. Let the pissing contest begin. "I'm a charter fisherman."

"Really?" He was now interested. "Then you must be fishing the tournament this weekend, no?"

"No, I am not."

He turned his head like a dog would when trying to understand English. "Oh, and why not?"

"I'm just not the tournament fishing kind of guy," I said. "I think the tournaments are hurting the—" Before I could spout another word, the guy I overheard earlier in the night swooped up to us.

Mr. Northwood turned to him. "There you are." He placed an arm on the man's back and introduced him as his son, Brant.

I noticed Brant's eyes went straight to Sara. She lowered her chin.

Mr. Northwood introduced us all, beginning with Cliff. Brant mentioned that he and Sara had already met.

"Brant's fishing the tournament this weekend," Mr. Northwood said. "Has a good jump on the competition," he boasted. "Been pre-fishing all week. Isn't that right, m'boy?" Graham had his hands in white pant pockets, rocking back on his heels, and then gave Brant an evocative elbow.

Brant replied, "Sure have … seen tons of big ol' bulls everywhere. In every sand hole and every dang creek." The way the guy spoke was as though he had already won the tournament. Winning the tournament, you were awarded a brand-new flats boat and a bunch of cash—solid motivation to cheat.

I excused myself courteously, acquired the last remaining buffet table, and proceeded to Cliff's van. I recognized the situation for what it was; it could have turned ugly if the conversation with Graham had continued. I'm not one to compromise Cliff's business.

At the van, I loaded the table and waited. A few minutes later, Cliff and Sara sauntered up.

I said to Cliff first, "You're a better man than me."

"Why do you say that?" Cliff said, adjusting my sloppy placement of the tables.

"Having to rub elbows with these people all night and keep a straight face. Impressive."

Cliff was now shifting piles of miscellaneous catering plates, cups, and silverware. "They're not that bad. Just got to tell 'em what they want to hear is all—networking."

"I guess."

Sara said, "Yeah, you left kinda quick."

"I didn't like the vibe that dude Brant was putting out."

"Vibe?" she questioned. "What do you know about *vibes*, *Mr. Pickford?*" She bumped her hips into mine, joyful of the raillery.

Bumping her back, I said, "I'd say I know *plenty* about *vibes.*"

She stuck her chin up. "Oh, yeah, prove it!"

"Well, I'm getting a *negative* vibe from you *right* now."

Cliff giggled.

"Negative?" she said. "I'll show you negative." She tried and succeeded at wiping leftover whipped cream across my face.

We said our goodbyes to Cliff and paced back to the truck.

****

The trip to Sara's Port Charlotte house was pleasant. The windows were down, flushing the Toyota cab with early summer air. An impressive acoustic version of *Doin' Time* by Sublime emitted from the radio. My eyes left the road on occasion and noticed Sara's impeccant glow as we passed streetlight after streetlight. She held her hand out the window and surfed the cool air over the Peace River. Sara doesn't play head games, nor is she out to conquer me. It's her simplicity—the kind that pulls no punches—that drew me in.

"So, what did you and *Brant* talk about?" I asked, emphasizing Brant.

"Really?" she said, but then muttered, "What a buzz killer..."

I smiled and blinked. "Just curious is all."

"We both know that's not true."

I looked forward, watching traffic, giving her a second to come around.

"Nothing," she said, "he called me over and wanted to say hi."

Truth was, I wasn't mad at Sara. I was being tested as a partner. It was clear to me that Brant, in my presence, had made a pass at Sara, even though it was obvious she wasn't single. So, I had to sprinkle a little hint of my awareness. "I'm not sure *that's* all he wanted..."

"Can't you just let it go?"

The real reason I pressed Sara wasn't about jealousy, but the notion of what Brant said at the party about the pens.

"Maybe," I said. "Did he mention the tournament?"

"I guess." She turned back to the window. "I wasn't really paying much attention."

I leveled with her. "The reason I'm asking is that he said something at the party. Kind of struck a nerve with me."

Sara, now skeptical and somewhat interested said, "Oh yeah? And what's that?"

"Well, I'm pretty sure I heard a whisper to one of his friends, and I quote, that 'The pens are set.'"

"Pens are set?"

"Yeah, it kind of stuck with me. He also said 'easy pickin's' and 'redfish magic.'"

"Are you thinking these two are up to something?"

"Yes," I answered. "I mean, then later Mr. Northwood elbowing his son after saying that 'he's got a jump on the competition.' That doesn't sound shady to you?"

She faced forward and reflected. "Yeah, I remember him doing that…"

"See, so it's not just me, then?"

Her expression turned serious. "Oh, it's you alright."

"Say what?"

"I think you're over-thinking this."

"Yeah, maybe you're right," I said, for her benefit.

****

We crossed the Barron Collier Bridge into Port Charlotte, a concrete link from Punta Gorda over the Peace River—known locally as the Punta Gorda Bridge.

Ahead of Sara's house, I killed the truck's engine, rolling it along the swale. The tires buzzed and vibrated through the floorboards.

"You working tomorrow?" I asked, squeaking the brakes to slow the truck to a stop.

"Yeah…" she said, rummaging through the glovebox. "I put my keys in here somewhere."

Since my departure from barnacle scraping, Sara had moved on with her career.

I shifted and faced her. She had found a Beardo—a knitted fake beard that attaches to a hat—an idea a friend suggested for when the temperature plummets during the winter months. Supposed to keep the face warm, making the cold winter runs across the harbor doable. I had forgotten about it, and it appeared Sara had fished it from the glovebox and was now wearing it.

"What is that?" I asked amusingly.

Even wearing the beard, she radiated a stunning glow.

"It looks good on you," I said.

She smiled, exposing an upper row scary straight teeth and leaned, stretching for a kiss—I didn't fight it.

I pushed her off playfully and wiped my mouth. "So, *that's* what it's like kissing someone with a beard?"

She shifted back to her seat and inspected herself in the visor mirror. She smiled to the mirror before pulling it off and returning it to the glovebox.

"Tomorrow, plans?"

"Nope, just running some errands."

"Finally cut the grass?"

"Now, I wouldn't go that far."

She laughed. "I didn't think so."

I shifted in my seat, turned toward her. "Funny. Hey, are you busy this weekend?"

"Umm … actually, my mom wants to go shopping for Debby's wedding."

"Your sister Debby?"

"You got it. Why?"

"Just wondering. Thinking I might take the boat and go check out the tournament."

She twirled a lock of her hair and then flicked it away from her face. "I figured you weren't going to let that go."

"Well, those guys are risking my livelihood. I depend on a healthy population of fish. If there is no fish, then there is no Shamus Pickford."

"I can understand that. I know how passionate you are about protecting the populations."

"Yeah, so…"

She leaned toward me again. "I just don't want you gettin' disappointed is all, Shamus. Sometimes you get worked up over all kinds of things, and sometimes they don't exactly pan out … yah know? Like, remember when you thought the garbage men were intentionally leaving the empty cans blocking your driveway?"

"They were!"

"Um, no … turned out to be a lift malfunction."

I turned away. "I don't know what you're talking about."

"Shamus."

Gave in, said, "I guess."

Her voice, softer now, and leaning closer, sent words along with her breath. "I know you're going do whatever you think is right … so you have *fun* doin' whatever you're plannin' on doin'." She kissed me. "But, please, and this is a big one. Please, don't do anything *stupid*, okay?"

"Okay," I answered.

"Promise?"

"Yes."

"Say it."

"I promise. Happy?"

Before I could speak another word, she levered open the door, swiveled out, and skipped up the driveway.

****

Back at the house, I opened the front door and Scupper sprang up, nearly knocking me to the ground—obviously smelling the steak and grouper I held high. At the counter, I reached in the cooler and lifted out a cold beer then stepped to the lanai with Scupper in a spastic trot. As I sat in a lawn chair and cracked open the top of the container, the intense aroma of meat and fish released from the dew-laden lid. I forked out a weighty piece of filet and slung it to Scupper—the grouper was mine.

While eating dinner in peace, I began thinking about the catering job, about the conversation I had overheard, and wondered if I take the 'pen' comment and combine it with the Graham situation, if it equaled anything significant. Perhaps an unfair advantage was taking place. I decided to text Cliff.

Hey, are you off Sat?

Ten minutes elapsed, then a reply.

Sure am.

Fish?

Let's do it!

Okay, be here at 6 a.m.

Will do.

Bring food.

I leaned back. Again, thoughts of my friend Klinger ran through my mind, and the psychological effects he had endured from the death of Eliot Waldrup. I hadn't seen him much, only a few brief times since the incident—and which none of them had been fishing. I often speculated about his whereabouts, and continued to invite him on fishing trips on a regular basis but I kept receiving the runaround— Mandy this, Mandy that... I decided to send him a text that read: *Just wanted to see if you're available to fish tomorrow? No pressure.*

****

The next day, Friday, I drove to the vet for Scupper's official check-up. I turned onto Burnt Store Road and faced north toward US41. *No Humans Veterinary Services*, for me, was the most convenient pet hospital in town. Another reason I might have chosen to take Scupper to it, was that I wanted to see an old lady friend of mine, Dr. Clara Hayes. Clara and I had somewhat of a blurry history. We tried dating, but early on, it became clear we wanted different things—so we ended whatever it was we had. Then, we did it all over again. It was always her call, and I never put up a fight.

Scupper began a frantic whine, raising her wet nose, swiping it against the half-down window. The pitch then rose to a strange level, in the same manner dogs do when they recognize home, behavior indicating she might've been to the vet before, and maybe this exact one.

The vet office had a unique smell—a combination of dog hair and scented carpet cleaner. In the waiting room, a grey-bearded, lumpy Doberman leashed by a woman greeted Scupper the way dogs do. Also waiting was a man cradling a pink, thin-haired pot-belly pig.

I signed in and sat, and my palms began to moisten. A fifty-five-gallon fish tank in the corner of the waiting room caught my attention, where tight schools of African cichlids swam in unison, and helped me to relax.

Fifteen minutes had ticked away before the young Dr. Clara appeared in the waiting room wearing a white lab coat. Her narrow forearm supported a brown clipboard. She was fresh out of college, having earned her veterinary degree by the age of twenty-seven. Her dark hair was pulled and tied to a tight ponytail. Bold, red-framed glasses rested halfway down her nose, protecting her acorn-colored eyes. Underneath the white lab coat were dark blue scrubs, top and bottoms, flattering the thin figure she hid. We made eye-contact, and she nodded me down the hallway.

"Hello, Shamus. Long time ... how have you been?"

"I've been good. You?"

"Oh, just wonderful." When she spoke, I couldn't tell whether it was sarcasm or genuine. Or maybe she said it that way on purpose. These were the games I missed.

Noticing Scupper, Dr. Clara knelt. "Oh, and who's this little girl?"

"Scupper. She's a stray I adopted." Scupper's tail was like a windshield wiper, slapping the narrow hallway walls.

I scratched Scupper's head. "I found her huddled underneath the front door awning. I noticed her around for a while, roaming the neighborhood. She was so skinny. I tried calling her to me. She was too scared, but then I started leaving food out for her, and she eventually came around."

"Well, Shamus," Dr Clara stood. "I have some news for you."

"Oh, yeah, what's that?" I pressed my moist palms together.

"By the looks of her, I'd say that her name is not Scupper, or whatever you are calling her."

I sensed bitterness in her tone.

Dr. Clara stepped into the hallway and called out, "Can you? Jen? Bring me the chip scanner?"

A minute later, a tall woman with lengthy, gray, knotted-tight dreadlocks, and wearing the same type scrubs, but with tiny dog treat emblems and no lab coat, handed Dr. Clara a scanning device. My eyes told me it was a racquetball racket, but instead of a net, nothing—just a hole.

Jen held the scanner, clutched a thick roll of skin before Scupper's shoulder and spread the scanner overtop. When it chirped out a short, high-pitched blip, Scupper flinched, trying furiously to lick the strange machine.

Dr. Clara read the display. "Yup, just as I suspected."

"What's that?" I wondered if the dog did indeed belong to someone else.

"Her name is not Scupper. It's Samantha."

I frowned. "Come again…?"

"Yup."

"She's been micro-chipped?"

"She sure has. About six months ago."

Now I asked the big question but wasn't so sure I wanted to hear the answer. "She doesn't belong to anyone, does she?"

"You can relax, Shamus. She doesn't belong to anyone, so you're safe." Until now, Dr. Clara had made little eye contact—but when she said this, she made earnest contact. People's pets were off limits. A professional courtesy I respected.

Keeping eye contact, I asked, "So, she's micro-chipped and has been named, but has no owner?"

Dr. Clara broke the eye contact. "That's exactly what I'm saying." She faced down to Scupper.

"Okay, then…"

Jen, who I assumed was a vet technician, spoke up. "This cutie is Samantha. She's a stray we kenneled awhile back and micro-chipped. She got loose one day, and we haven't seen her since. Very clever dog you've got here, yah."

"Really?" I said, feeling somewhat relieved.

Jen perched up both of Scupper's ears and scratched. "Yup. We had her for about two weeks. She was wandering around, sniffing behind the hospital near the kennel cages, yah. Instead of running after her, we left one of the cages open and she walked right in."

I asked, "I wonder how she made it all the way across town to my neighborhood? It's like six miles away."

"It's common for stray dogs to wander great distances, even in just one afternoon," Jen explained. "Most of the time they follow their noses, yah."

Dr. Clara let her assistant continue explaining while she lifted the dog onto the stainless-steel examining table. She used the stethoscope earpieces to swipe a loose strand of floating hair away from her ears and inserted the small, pearly tips. She timed the beats using a watch while listening carefully to Scupper's heart. Once satisfied, she removed a small digital thermometer from a drawer next to the sink. Scupper's ears perked and straightened as Dr. Clara inserted it up the pup's ass.

Feeling to defend the pup, I spoke to the both: "How did she get loose … from here?" I said, but sent subliminal, lighthearted blame directed at Dr. Clara.

Jen jumped in. "She escaped through a small hole she dug under the cages. Smart dog here, yah. She'd dig a little at a time—then used toys and sticks to cover it, and when no one was paying attention, she'd continue. Pretty clever."

"Yes, it is," I said, and looked Scupper in her brown eyes. "How did you do that?"

Her tan tail wagged, as if understanding.

Dr. Clara said with little patience, "I'd say you have a healthy pet here, Shamus. Is there anything else I can help you with?"

Before I answered, someone called Jen into another room.

"Nope, so … what's the charge?" I said. "What do I owe yah?"

She was rinsing off the thermometer in the sink and didn't look up. "Now, you didn't have any money back when—" She paused, seemed careful in her word choice. "Well, you remember. Let's just call it even?"

Wow, I thought. "No, I insist. I want to pay."

"Okay," she said, impressed. "I'll send you the bill. I assume you're still out off Burnt Store Road?"

"Sure am."

Dr. Clara finished washing the thermometer and put it in a drawer, made eye contact, and told me, "It was good to see you." She exited the room while leaving me to find my own way out.

I lowered Scupper to the floor and proceeded down the hallway, passing the next examining room. Dr. Clara was speaking compassionately to the Doberman's owner.

The reception area had gotten crowded, and as I went for the door, a voice behind me called, "Shamus? Wait a minute, yah?"

It was Jen waving the micro-chip scanner. "Let's get this chip updated, shall we?"

"Thanks, that would be helpful," I said.

She swiped the scanner overtop Scupper's neck and waited for a beep. She asked me my name and address, then typed it on the digital screen, and again waved the device across Scupper. The machine made a longer beep.

"All set."

"Thanks, Jen … I really appreciate it."

"No problem at all. Take care of our old friend, yah?"

"Will do."

In the parking lot, I guided Scupper to a small patch of dead grass, unleashed her, and she did her business. I began wondering what the meaning of Dr. Clara's bitterness was. She ended each time, so her attitude didn't compute. I would've been more than willing to continue whatever it was we had.

After Scupper finished, she followed me to the truck and balanced on the passenger seat. I returned to US41. There was one more stop I needed to make before heading to the house.

We drove north once Scupper and I reached US41, passing the Punta Gorda Boat Ramp—ground zero for the tournament—and crossed into Port Charlotte using the Punta Gorda Bridge. On the Port Charlotte side, I rolled into a dirt parking lot at the base of the bridge called Live Oak Point, which saw most of its use from patrons who utilized the bridge for walking, running, and fishing mostly. The truck trundled along, tires spun, crackling overtop the bright, white dirt. Scupper's ears flicked stiff as she watched men fish from the bridge. My truck glided to a stop

I slipped out my cell phone and dialed my old friend Donny Elrod. Along with a few others in high school, we'd fished the Boca Grande phosphate dock more times than I could count—well, before it had been wrecked, dismantled, and restricted from land-based fishing, leaving only dozens of rotting pilings.

Donny was smart, and after high school graduation, he decided on finding a real job. I, on the other hand, didn't—although I failed to see who was smarter at the time. Donny agreed to stop and chat.

Out of boredom, I snapped the leash on Scupper's fishtail-symbolled collar and let her nose lead us through the park. She spotted a fisherman cranking a reel with a bent rod tip. "A fish," I said.

Scupper guided me along the cracked and river-eroded seawall to the fisherman. Her nose poked at the head of the caught fish. The catfish slapped its tail on the concrete seawall and Scupper snapped back, instinctually aware of the danger the barbs may pose. Now prone, the catfish used spiny pectoral fins-like elbows, crawling toward the seawall lip, leaving a trail of slime. It was fascinating that the fish knew its one hope of survival was managing to get to the edge of the seawall.

The fisherman smiled, exposing a single, corn-colored lower tooth. He laughed at Scupper's curiosity, as if a child hearing a joke for the first time—a simple man no doubt. His green, paint-splattered jean shorts hung below a white underwear-exposed waist. The yellow, collared shirt had been splashed with identical green paint, and his underarm had multiple sweat-stained rings. His hair, long and frizzy, fumed a steaming pungent odor of spoiled laundry. His beard grew gray, except for the red-brown stains rimming his mouth.

He kicked the catfish into the sand. "She dinner." He then tensed up, straightening his body, turned, and then cast his line out using all his might.

My friend arrived in a county-issued work truck and parked beside my pickup. I didn't like to call in favors, but I knew Donny would share my enthusiasm for this matter, and he had full access to the restricted data I required. Despite his line of work, Donny was approaching four hundred pounds. His head was shaved shiny, with a black halo of male pattern baldness. Clean-shaven, his face had a boyish smoothness that contrasted oddly with his sparkling upper veneers and six-foot-four-inch frame.

I grinned, held out my hand. "What's up, man?"

"Not much," answered Donny. "Just on break."

"Cool, cool."

We shook and Scupper sniffed Donny's shiny black shoes.

It'd been a few months since I'd seen him, so I asked about Brenda, his girlfriend.

"You mean fiancée?" he corrected.

"Congratulations, man," I said. "What made you decide to take the big ol' leap?"

"Well, we've been together for some time," he explained. "She's been hinting at it for little while now, so…"

"I see, and you did the right thing because you ain't ever gonna find another woman like Brenda," I said. "Especially with your ugly mug."

He appreciated the levity and grinned. "You ain't kidding, Shamus." He shoved my shoulder. "What up with you? You got a girl yet, or still living that bachelor lifestyle everyone's envious of?"

"No, not anymore," I explained. "I've been dating a wonderful woman—Sara. It started out as an employer, employee relationship, but developed quickly into something more serious."

"Oh, yeah?"

"Yeah, she's a great girl."

"So, somebody was able to tame the *great* Shamus *Pickford?*"

"Tame is kinda a strong word—"

He cut me off and peered toward the suspicious fisherman. "What's this guy's deal?"

"Oh, he's no problem, just a fisherman minding his own business—probably tryin' to catch some dinner."

"Sure does look rough."

"Yeah. He's probably homeless."

"You might be right," Donny replied.

We continued watching the man for a few extra seconds. Donny really eyeballed the guy. The fisherman seemed to sense Donny sizing him up and turned his head.

I snagged his attention back. "Hey, the reason I wanted to meet is I need a favor."

"Anything, bud. What yah got for me?"

My eyes slanted. "Do you still have access to that *trove* of information?"

"You mean the one in the work vehicle?"

"Yes," I answered. "That's the one."

"Yeah, I still got access to it." Donny returned to me and spoke in earnest. "What you need?"

"I was wondering if you could search something for me. It's probably nothing, but it might give be a better idea of whom I'm going to deal with."

Donny straightened up and folded his arms. "Somebody givin' you trouble? If they are you just tell me and—"

"No, no. It's nothing like that." I placed my hand onto his shoulder. "I just overheard something that I can't let go."

"Not surprising with you," he said. Donny knew me well, and he knew I didn't like leaving situations unresolved. Anal retentive, maybe?

I warned, "In a second you might not be able to let it go either..."

"What happened?" He became skeptical. "Some old fart hit on your new girlfriend or something?"

"No," I said. "Nothing like that."

"Well, dang. You got me all chubbed up ... let's hear it already."

"Okay, okay. You know that tournament this weekend?"

"The big redfish one? Who doesn't? Biggest one of the year."

I nodded. "How would you feel if I had information that would lead us to believe that a team is conspiring to acquire a not-so-legal advantage?"

"What you sayin'? Like cheat or somethin'?"

"Yes—given they had the opportunity."

Donny face twisted into an uncertain frown. "How you gonna cheat those fishing tournaments? They got spotters out there watching all the teams, every which way. Can't even take a piss without them seeing yah. They watch every move, where you go and how far you travel ... kinda hard these days."

"That's correct."

Donny leaned in. "Plus, don't forget about the *big* one."

Confused, I fell for the bait. "And what's that?"

Donny looked me straight in the eyes. "The lie detector test, remember? First place gotta take one."

"That's right," I said, surprised. "I forgot about that. Kinda hard to fake one of those."

Donny went ominous. "Lie detector tests doesn't mean squat though. I know firsthand people can *easily* pass those."

"This is true." I paused, soaking in the realization of which Donny had just laid on me. I went on and explained, "But what I'm saying is, if this team in question were to cheat, if the opportunity presented itself to them, and you knew about *that* opportunity, would *you* be able to let it go?"

"Depends," he answered.

"Depends on what?" I asked.

He half-grinned, an expression that had to be earned—a semblance filled with history and meaning—an understanding reserved for old friends that took years to develop. "Depends on if I'm the only one that knows about it or not."

"Let's just say that I'm pretty damn sure I'm the only one who knows about it. Well, except for Cliff, of course."

"Cliff Fleming?"

"Yes, we were together when the whole thing came to light."

"Okay, so, what happened, bubba?" He re-crossed his arms, tasted the air like a snake, and said, "I'm all ears."

After explaining what I overheard, Donny agreed to search the information for me.

Sitting in the driver's seat, leaning over, he typed away at the green computer screen. "Okay, what's the last name?"

"Northwood," I said.

"You said first name was Brant?"

"Yeah."

I stood, craning over his shoulder as the information queried on the screen. Warmth from underneath the truck rose, sending up a wave of heat, fogging out my sunglasses.

My old friend scrolled through the listings flashing on the screen. "Let's see…"

Endless rows of meaningless data streamed past me.

He asked, "I have a couple of people by that name. Do you know the address?"

"I believe he lives on Palm Tree Drive."

Donny kept searching, tapping the square mouse pad, clicking here, clicking there.

The fisherman was keeping an unobstructed sightline, monitoring from his peripheral vision. His head turned as he noticed me watching.

After a few idle minutes, Donny sprang alive. "Here we go."

"Found him?"

He rotated the laptop lying across his legs, giving me a better view of the photo. "Looks like this guy's cleeeean as a whistle."

"Yeah, that's him all right," I said. "Blond hair … goofy smirk. Clean, huh?"

"Yeah, not even a parking ticket."

"Try this name real quick?" I asked. "If you don't mind."

"Fire away."

"Try Graham Northwood. That's his shady father."

"No problem," Donny replied while he typed away.

"Just a hunch."

"Well, *this* guy has a bit of a history."

"Oh, yeah … like?" I glanced closer, squinting at the computer screen, but the sun's glare distorted my view.

"Only like a few traffic tickets."

"How far back does this system go? I mean, how far back can you search?"

"Seven years," he answered.

I scratched my head and wondered if I'd missed anything. Donny clicked his finger and continued scrolling for information.

I thought about Graham's profession. "Does it say what kind of business Graham Northwood is in?"

"Yes, it has one profession listed, and that's 'entrepreneur.'"

"Kinda vague, could mean many things," I said. "I figured it would be a long-shot finding anything substantial. I mean … they must have a reason to cheat, right?"

Donny said, "I bet if you find out what this dude is entrepreneur-*ing*, then I say you find your motive."

"I think you're right."

I cleared back from the truck as Donny snapped the laptop closed. He got out and shut the door.

"Well, so far, seems both guys are clean," he noted, adjusting his pants.

"It appears so."

He tightened his belt. "I mean … what did you expect to find? A long history of cheating at fishing tournaments?"

"Yeah, I guess you're right… I might have been reaching on this one."

Donny patted me on the back. "Didn't hurt to try, right?"

Scupper sniffed Donny's shoes again.

My friend pointed out, "This Brant guy … I mean, he might not even be up to anything. You could just be acting paranoid."

"That's what Sara suggested last night."

"I thought you said only you and Cliff knew about it?" Donny was always on top of details.

"She knows, too," I shrugged, "…but thinks I'm crazy."

"But don't let that stop you from going out tomorrow and trailing these guys." His brow now rose. "You know … just in case."

"Oh, don't worry about that. Cliff and I are heading out early."

The sun was beating down rays of sweltering heat. Scupper sat on my foot panting, tongue hanging, ears perked at another dog barking in the distance.

Donny wiped sweat from his forehead. "I'd better get going now. Back to workin' for the man…"

"Okay, thanks for helping me out. I owe you one."

"No problem. Let me know what you find tomorrow." Donny climbed back into his work truck, suspension straining from the weight, and pulled away.

I let Scupper jump into the cab of my truck but first waved a friendly goodbye to the fisherman.

Chapter Three

Saturday morning came along soon, and as usual Cliff arrived on time. He knew me all too well, including my disposition toward tardiness. His brand-new Chevy truck rolled up the driveway.

I had just brewed a pot of fresh Mexican coffee and headed out to the garage to greet Cliff. The morning air was crisp, like the first pages of a new book, but a weak sense of rain covered the sky in slight, over-casting clouds. I wondered if Mother Nature would keep herself composed today so that we could accomplish our mission.

A path of re-purposed construction concrete, fifty feet long, separated the garage from the house.

I offered Cliff a cup of coffee—as I do to all my morning fishing guests.

"I'd love some." Cliff was dressed in green, light-weight fishing attire, except for his thick, cotton ball-topped red winter hat.

"So, that's your new truck," I said. "Looks real clean."

He smiled. "It *is* clean, brother. Brand new."

"I don't even want to know what you paid for it."

He sniffed. "It wasn't too bad."

I said, "I know you. You don't buy cheap trucks."

We both admired it. "Got a hell of a deal on it," he said.

I grinned. "Just don't call me when the computers and tiny motors that run everything start failing and you break down somewhere."

"You and your anti-technology…"

"I'm not *completely* anti-technology." I circled the Chevy. "I'm just not a fan of technology that makes humans lazier and dumber than they already are. Like automatic locks—useless. Is sticking in a key *that* hard?"

He pointed out, "No, but it's nice being able to call customer service and have them remotely open the doors if you lose your key or lock them inside."

"That's the point. It allows complacency on responsibility."

"I can start it from inside the house," he said. "During cold winter mornings, comes in handy."

"Okay, you win. Let us get coffee."

As we walked along the path to the front door, Cliff hit the lock button on the key fob, honking the horn twice and flashing the truck's lights.

"Nice." I half-turned to see his shit-eating grin.

Scupper raked up her front paws, acknowledging Cliff's immediate first steps into the house.

"Down, girl," I said. "She's still kinda rambunctious."

"It's cool," he said. "You tiled the kitchen walls … not bad, not bad."

"Yeah." My house was a work in progress and maybe its incompleteness served as a metaphor for my own life, mirroring my journey in a way that encouraged progress. It was something simple to accomplish—a goal, perhaps a finished project, and then a personal goal fulfilled.

I poured a fresh cup into a mini thermal mug. "I'm taking a traveler."

At the garage, we selected our gear and made way to the dock. Still dark, the sun had yet to rise, though it seemed to press at the horizon. With each passing second, visibility sharpened, and in a blink, dawn appeared.

Cliff commented on my path as we walked. "You can barely see over the grass."

"I know—it's getting out of hand. I need to call Klinger over here and cut it."

He offered, "Shoot, I'll cut it for the right price."

I asked, "Do you know anyone that owns a horse? Or a cow?"

"Why? You want to borrow one, to come eat the grass?"

"That's not a bad idea, but I meant to *bail* it up, and then *take* it away."

"I bet a few goats will have this gone in no time," he said.

"Then I'd have goat shit everywhere."

"Better than horse shit."

I almost erupted into laughter. "Okay, do you know any goats?"

A ten-foot plank I'd laid from the seawall to the dock was the best way of crossing—and I wouldn't say safely. As I stepped out, Cliff noticed it wobbling more than usual.

"This thing gonna hold us?" he said.

"It should, but we won't know until you step on it."

I watched intently as the half-rotted rim joists wobbled, and the waist-high railing shook as he stepped. As he transferred his weight to the dock, the sea grape leaves beside it began shifting like spider legs.

Due to recent repairs, the skiff's engine was running good as new. After the nightmare at the Turtle Bay fish shack, the skiff reeked of fuel. I had the mechanic replace the front baitwell and run new lines, but the smell lingered. So did the memory. Each time I stepped aboard, that day came rushing back. Cliff was one of my oldest friends, and still, I couldn't bring myself to tell him everything.

All he knew was that Klinger and I heard gunshots and then went to investigate. What we found was a man bleeding to death. To this day, nobody knew about the plane, crate, or the money. The police investigation concluded that it had been a murder. One man shot another out of rage. The killer tried to escape, but ran overtop an oyster bed, and soon after, eaten by wild hogs. One day, sure, I'll tell him, but now the only people who know, or need to know, are the involved parties—Klinger, the missing Flip, and me.

Cliff untied the dock line, and I pushed us off alongside the houseboat.

Making way, Spinner assumed its normal arching positioning beside the boat. For safety reasons, I switched on the red and green running lights.

Cliff noticed Spinner. "Oh, cool. You got it trained to swim right next to the boat?"

"Nope, it just started doing it on its own. Each time I crank up the engine, it shows up and guides me out."

Cliff stretched and tried to pet it. "That's cool as hell."

"Yeah, it is, isn't it?"

We passed Flip's mid-60s built house, and still no one appeared to be home. His overgrown grass tangled as awkwardly as mine, so it felt abandoned.

"Tide looks good," Cliff said, sitting on the cushion ahead of the console.

"Yeah, it's coming in. Should be high around noon."

Half-submerged clusters of oyster beds stretched across the center of the basin. Sunlight remained scarce, but the air was warming. So far, so good as Spinner followed behind, letting out a long, echoing *pooooeeeesh*.

Cliff bit from a breakfast cheese stick. "So, what's the plan?"

"Pretty simple, I think. Follow these turds until they lead us to the pen."

Half-turned around, and asked, "Follow him? He'll definitely notice us then."

"We must be sly about it, unidentified … but I think noticing us is fine."

"Gotcha—makes sense."

"Remember, Brant won't be expecting us," I explained. "He doesn't have a reason to suspect that we're following him. Plus, we can always use our *Buffs* as cover, and he'll never know who we are."

"Has he ever seen your skiff?"

I shook my head. "Nope."

"So, if we catch him actually pulling redfish out of a trap, are we gonna just run up on him?"

"Good question," I said. "And no, we're not. I'll take pictures and let him process through weigh-ins. If he wins or takes home any prizes, I'll be ready to confront him then."

"Gotcha. For a better reveal. Let everyone witness him getting caught."

I grinned. "Yup."

"Gonna turn him in?" he asked.

"I'd like to but under no circumstances is Shamus Pickford a rat. No way."

Cliff smiled and sunk into thought.

At a slow idle, the boat ride from the dock to the inlet took five minutes. It wasn't a bad start to the day. For most of my life, these morning boat rides were a much-needed preamble, a loan of time, allowing me to enjoy a coffee and shake the fogginess from my brain.

"What's the start time for the tourney?" Cliff asked as we exited the basin.

"I think it's around seven o'clock."

"About six-thirty right now, I think." He pulled out a cell phone, checking the time. "Yup, six twenty-eight."

"We'd better get going."

Cliff was no stranger to my anal-retentive ways and maneuvered into his launch position. And after Spinner was nowhere in sight, I hit the throttle, bursting the skiff with harmless speed, increasing the RPMs to a comfortable three thousand.

As of late, I questioned the dolphin's reluctance to follow me past the mouth of the basin. It almost gave me a look, same as when I left Scupper when I go on charter.

The skiff rode level atop the still water, its engine—fresh from a tune-up—purring with a low, balanced vibration.

Ahead in the dim light, a large flock of pelicans hovered in patience above the water, searching for the first bright reflection of light to unleash a violent neck stab into the ball of baitfish.

We headed toward the northeast rim of Charlotte Harbor. The tournament was set to begin at the boat ramp alongside the Punta Gorda Bridge. From the flats outside the basin, it was a thirty-minute boat ride.

The eastern wall of Charlotte Harbor, as far as time might tell, had always been stacked with narrow winding creeks, tiny mangrove islands, and endless hidden oyster beds. From the tip of Two Pines to a tick north of Whore House Point was backcountry at its finest. One could fish for years and still have oodles of undiscovered areas to explore.

We moved through shifting pockets of cool morning air. In a few more weeks, they'd be gone and replaced by the heavy heat of summer. The ride so far went un-conversational. There's something inherently meditative about a boat ride—its rhythm suited for reflection, its silence designed to untangle and rework a burdened conscience.

Twenty minutes in, we glided over the shallow flat south of Alligator Creek and crossed the channel, marked unmistakably by the weathered old water tower visible from every corner of the harbor. After passing the iconic water tower, we crossed Poachers Cut, rounded Whore House Point, and traversed the shallow flats outside Ponce de Leon Park, eager for the Punta Gorda Bridge.

Cliff pointed to an impressive rooster tail, shouted over the engine, "I think they're letting the first of the boats go."

"Yeah, seems we're a bit late."

"Only a few have left though."

Rooter tails were fun to awe at, but then you realize what you're witnessing was a two hundred and fifty-horsepowered meathead. For safety, tournament officials gave each boat a random draw number, and a time to be released individually. This helped prevent collisions from the zealous-to-fish participants. As we rounded the Colony Point Condos, I brought the boat back to idle speed and off plane.

I peered toward the Punta Gorda Bridge on a fast float. Cliff pulled out an ultra-light spinning rod and flung a few casts along the seawall.

The starting point for the tournament was a local fishing pier between I-75 and the Punta Gorda Bridge. Each boat passed a series of check-in stages. Once they passed the last checkpoint, a green light signaled completion and off they went. The wooden-bumpered channel underneath the center of the bridge was an IDLE ZONE but had little effect on over-anxious speeding boats. The bridge pilings on opposite sides of the channel offered plenty of depth and appeared to be the chosen route—kind of a boater loophole.

As we sat, every two minutes a boat barreled out from under the bridge, passing Fisherman's Village and crossing our path.

Cliff seemed confused. "How are we going to tell which boat this guy is on?"

"With these." I reached inside the center console and removed a brand-new pair of binoculars. After the sorrowful incident involving Eliot at the fish shack, I invested in my own pair. I rested them on the bridge of my nose, then adjusted the focus and scanned for boats.

Cliff saw me using the binoculars. "They look serious."

After weaving through the anchored liveaboards off Gilchrest Park, I tracked a passing boat through the lenes. "They're not bad, but I'm not sure this will work. Even zooming in, their hats and sunglasses kind of block their faces."

Cliff suggested, "Since only a few boats have been released from the start, why not go underneath one of those bridge sections?" He leveled up a finger toward the bridge, an area closer to land, and the starting point. "We could just sit and wait. He ain't gonna recognize us from there."

Cliff had a point. Our spot wasn't ideal for tracking, and I couldn't see faces, and neither one of us knew what type of boat Brant was on. I handed the binoculars to Cliff and asked if he would keep an eye on the boats while we motored under the bridge. He agreed.

We inched our way to the Punta Gorda Bridge, idling parallel along the seawalls, leading past the prestigious Iles of Punta Gorda. Cliff had been scanning each boat for Brant, the tall blond, and possibly a crew of equally unsuspecting bros.

Boat after boat shot past—Lake 'n Bays, Hewes Redfishers, Action Crafts, Low Tides, and more Pathfinders than I could count.

"He must've had a high draw number," Cliff noted. A draw number was assigned at random during the captain's meeting the day before the tournament. It determined the order of departure—boat number one leading the pack at launch.

"How many boats is this so far?" I asked Cliff.

Cliff had the binoculars pressed up to his eyes. "Man, it's probably been, um, at least fifty by now."

Fifty boats was a good turnout for any fishing tournament. Charlotte Harbor hosts a fishing tournament often during the early spring months, continuing through late summer, early September. Not every tournament targeted redfish, which was a species in decline. Why there was no season on them, I'll never know.

My frustration mounted. Failing to identify the right boat sparked a restless storm of thoughts. Sooner rather than later, it seemed wise to try a new tactic. As the sun made its morning debut, I decided that getting a bit closer to the starting pier would gain the visibility we desired.

Cliff lowered the binoculars from his eyes and shook his head. "I'm not sure how many have left now."

"Yeah, me either," I said. "Let's go toward the pier and scope out the last remaining boats. Never know…"

"It's your call."

I tapped the throttle, increasing the skiff's speed to a soft plane. We motored under the Punta Gorda Bridge and breezed ahead of the Charlotte County Convention Center. After Hurricane Charley, the old Memorial Auditorium was torn down. In its replacement the new convention center had just about disabled the seawall fishing that many people had, throughout the years, very much enjoyed.

A short line of five boats were bobbing patiently along the metal-railed pier.

A sense of urgency filled Cliff's tone. "Hey, does that look like him?"

He handed me the binoculars, and I focused on the pier. "Which one are you talking about?"

"Third one from the end—the twenty-two-foot towered Pathy."

"Oh, yeah, I see it now."

Cliff stood confidently next me. "Looks like him to me."

"I think you're right," I said. "His little sidekick from the party is also aboard."

For reasons beyond me, Brant remained nearly dead last, left waiting at the end of the line where Both men dressed identically in matching cobalt fishing shirts and loud Hawaiian-themed board shorts. Their team's name should have been labeled somewhere on their jerseys, but even as I squinted through the helpful binoculars, it was too far to confirm. His boat appeared to be a towered 22v Pathfinder Tournament Edition, painted in a phosphorus-green hull. Towered flats boats were indeed nice, and more importantly, allowed a fresh vantage point into the surrounding waters that extend visibility, and weren't cheap.

"Talk about luck," I said.

Cliff grinned. "Meant to be...?"

"Is that a three hundred Yamaha on the back?"

"Sure appears so." Cliff sat admiring. "I bet it hauls ass."

"That could be a problem," I said. "We have no chance of staying on him, as far as speed goes. That boat probably runs about sixty or so with that over-powered motor."

Cliff scoffed. "Shoot, I was thinking seventy."

I handed Cliff the binoculars. "Let's keep an eye on it and see where he goes. Now we know what boat he's on, we can back off a bit. See if you can make out team names..."

I squinted to see the men prepare for launch. Sadly, their engine cranking out three hundred horsepower would leave us eating his wake. They passed the checkpoints and arrived at the final stage.

"We should get a small jump on him," I said.

I rode the boat on a half-plane, coasting underneath the Punta Gorda Bridge. In short gusts, the wind induced short ripples overtop the water.

Once we swept under the bridge, I hammered the boat on a full-out plane, and we cut back through the Fisherman's Village channel markers. Cliff was focused behind us, keeping his eyes on Brant.

"You still see them?" I asked.

"Sure do, brother." The binoculars were pressed up to his eyes. "He's just going under the bridge now, in the channel."

We cruised on plane, passing Gilchrest Park the opposite way, and then the canal inlets leading into Punta Gorda Isles.

At Colony Point, onlookers used binoculars too, peering out from their high-rise, high-priced condos. I understood the excitement. To see multiple rooster tails must be an engrossing scene for the retiree. I waved at them—a sort of wave that might have said: "I'll take care of it" or "I'm on it," and depending on who was up there, determined the civility of a returned wave. Some people were against all tournament action, desiring quiet and peacefulness. Those people wouldn't wave back. Others loved the tournament for its profits, the boost it brought to local businesses, and the small benefit—if any—it provided to the local economy. It's been proven that when money gets involved, the environment always loses.

To decide our next move, I aimed toward Ponce de Leon Park and the surrounding flats.

As we hit the bar, slapping overtop numerous sand holes, the mixing of fresh and saltwater from up the Peace River gave the water an interesting glow—a demarcation of water types as tea-colored water below blended into cherry red tints. We crossed the channel markers and settled off plane.

Cliff peered at Brant and Co. "Those guys are movin'...'"

I zoomed in, sighting to no avail, but then saw the silhouette of a distant tower boat—might've been anyone—not the phosphorus green hull of the intended Pathfinder.

At Ponce de Leon Park, cars had begun filling the vacant parking slots. Ponce, what the locals call it, spreads ten acres in size and was a mid-harbor launch site for boaters, providing quick access for those who seek Charlotte Harbor's backcountry. It was where The Peace River Wildlife Center was located and features a quarter mile boardwalk through beautiful coastal wetlands. But the continuous boat traffic made Ponce a delicate place to fish.

A single fisherman wheeled his fishing cart toward the boat ramp, gripping the shiny metal railing attached to the pier. Sunlight glistened off it, and easing her way up, the sun sent the first few beams of heat our way.

"Still got the bead on them?" I asked Cliff.

"Yeah, and they'll be rounding Ponce in about two minutes."

"Okay, just don't lose them."

Cliff headed to the bow, binoculars in hand. "Here they come." He then shouted, "See them?" and slung two fingers militarily toward the center of the harbor. "Can't miss that tower … looks like two people sitting up in it."

"Yeah, I see them," I answered.

"Doesn't appear like they're headed to the Myakka Cutoff, though. If they were headed to it, they sure would have changed course by now."

Cliff was correct again, the boat had crossed the mouth of the Myakka Cutoff, a

tell-tale sign they might cross the harbor. I didn't desire to cross the choppy, intimidating white-capped harbor in a lightweight, sixteen-foot-eight-inch skiff. Thankfully, right now, the chop appeared to be a manageable one, two-foot peak. To offer ourselves a chance, speed wise, we had to move now if we were to keep with Brant and his crew.

Cliff assumed the launch position, and I blasted the boat on plane.

Chapter Four

Halfway across the harbor, we still had Brant in our sights, but he'd gained a sizable lead.

After a good twenty minutes, we followed along the sandbar paralleling the West Wall as Brant's boat slowed, then idled along the mangroves three hundred yards. Cliff noticed it too.

"Bait," he said. "Shouldn't take them very long. Pelicans divin' everywhere."

"Yeah, we'd better stay back here a few minutes … just in case."

Cliff was on to something, so we sat on the bar, bobbing up and down like a couple of row-boaters.

"That's fine," I said. "Just keep an eye on those guys. That rig'll get them gone quick."

"Will do," he replied, and knelt on the front deck like a hunting dog.

I asked, "Are those guys using a cast net?"

His voice muffled through the tarpon-scale *Buff*. "No, the smaller dude is standing on the deck in a scouting position … leaning forward."

It didn't surprise me that they'd carved out time to catch bait. Most local fishing tournaments allowed either live bait or artificial lures. But due to its difficulty, not every fisherman was skilled at tossing lures.

Cliff handed me the binoculars.

As we idled the shallow water caused drag and pull to the skeg. I raised it using the jack plate.

"They're getting ready to take off." I raised my voice. "We better get going."

I aimed the binoculars towards the Pathfinder and focused the image. It appeared Brant and Co. also had their engine tilted, and they were circling—indicating Brant had begun searching for a deep hole, one that held enough water to launch on plane. When they found it, they did just that.

"We need to go … they're almost out of sight."

Planing out in a shallow corridor like this was no easy task. It took precision to hit the sweet spot where power met lift. Hitting the throttle formed a small whirlpool behind the engine. For balance and habit, I gripped the stainless-steel wheel tight as I mashed the trim tabs to lower the bow. As the water began to clear, the skiff settled on a smooth plane.

Along the shore, we passed strips of white, long-dead mangroves and tangles of sea grass. An angry thunderstorm had swept through three nights prior, practically opening the roof of my house like a can of sardines. No surprise the mangrove bank had been modified with scattered debris.

Ahead, a small blip of the Pathfinder was visible. They'd aimed toward Cape Haze Peninsula, skimming overtop a light chop. Unless they slowed, we wouldn't catch them.

My sixty-horsepower engine pushed us along at a respectable thirty miles an hour while short gusts rocked the bow. Upgrading to a larger boat only crossed my mind when dealing with Charlotte Harbor's bloodthirsty winds.

Charlotte Harbor's West Wall was seven nautical miles long—from Cattle Dock Point to Cape Haze Point and held a handful of small creeks and deep-water corridors—all of which were anchoring two or three boats each. The tournament had spawned crowded fishing at its best. Same as the annual tarpon tournaments that take place in Boca Grande Pass, and where normally courteous, decent-minded guides, seem to temporarily bypass proper boating etiquette, all for the prestige of catching a winning silver king.

We skimmed past most clusters of boats. I recognized a few. Some were friends who might recognize my skiff. After three miles, I had counted twenty boats.

Above the engine, Cliff half-turned and shouted, "I've never seen so many boats out here."

"I know, right? Because the prizes are *big* this year."

"I hear they're giving away a new flat's boat this year," he said.

"Yeah, it's a voucher for a new Hewes Redfisher."

Cliff paused in thought, leisurely facing forward.

Knowing that cell phone coverage was about to end, I pulled out my cell, and read the screen.

Missed message from Sara.

While still cruising at thirty miles per hour, I revealed her message. *I hope your day is going well, and you better not be doing anything STUPID!*

It wasn't easy, but I replied: *Don't worry, won't! Can you go by the house, let Scupper out? If you have time?*

I hit send.

The Pathfinder, at this point, had all but disappeared. As expected, Brant's three hundred horsepower had gotten the best of my skiff, but we pressed on. Dozens of boats overcrowded the West Wall, so the backcountry was Brant's likely destination—to where I knew best.

Chapter Five

After counting ten to fifteen additional boats, Cliff and I arrived outside Cape Haze Peninsula in a small channel between two mangrove tips. I'd fished this point dozens of times after the incident involving the Turtle Bay fish shack, and it still chills me, haunted by a false stench of decaying roadkill. Lester Smith's whole body had never been found, just skull remnants and a gun.

I never told Cliff or anyone about that day. Sometimes, though, I'd like to talk to someone I trusted, but the time wasn't right. Klinger, Flip, and I had made a solemn promise to remain silent, and I intended to honor that.

Once in the protection of the channel, I brought the skiff off plane and deadened the engine.

"What are you thinking?" Cliff asked.

"I'm not sure," I said, discouraged. "Brant's boat is too fast for us. I think we lost them—or they lost us?"

"I bet they were topping sixty-miles per hour."

"I'd have to agree. According to the GPS, my skiff tops out at thirty-three miles per hour, and they were running at least twice that."

I opened the cooler and snagged a water bottle and stepped to the bow. "I'm not so sure they'd travel all the way to Boca Grande—I mean, it's possible, I guess."

"Bet they went back in Bull Bay," Cliff said. "You know how much area that is to cover?"

"I suppose we could motor around, maybe get lucky?"

"True..."

I pondered a minute. "We need to catch them in the act. I mean, that's our *only* chance."

We sat floating for a few silent minutes. I then noticed a boater tucked into a narrow, neighboring mangrove pocket. "You see those guys over there?" I asked Cliff, nodding toward the boat's general direction.

He turned. "Yeah, I see them."

"They're sitting on top of one of my new honey holes."

Cliff cupped his eyes to get a better view. "Fishing?"

"I'm not sure, but I don't think they saw us pull in, because they just tried signaling to a passing boat."

"Really?"

"Watch them for a minute," I said. "Wait for the next boat to pass."

Five minutes later, "Here comes one," Cliff said.

As the boat passed, one of the men waved.

"See?" I said.

"Yeah—nobody wants to stop," Cliff noted. "I'm pretty sure they don't even know we are here."

I snatched the push pole and nudged the skiff, gliding us against the wind and into clear sight. They saw us and waved.

I didn't see any registration decals, but the boat was in rough shape. It appeared to be an old sixteen-foot no-name skiff—the inside filthy, maybe doubling as a crabbing skiff. The wooden console had cracked gauges and exposed spliced wires. The entire deck was sky blue. The engine cowling was off resting in a puddle of mucky water. It was being steered by frayed stainless rotary cables, leading to a duct-taped black composite wheel.

The older of the two men was short and sickly skinny. He was wearing a worn thin banana-colored fishing shirt and a floppy-eared fishing hat sat cockeyed on his head. His face was white, smeared in oily sunscreen. He also wore khaki fishing shorts, revealing varicose-veined legs. The younger of the two I'd guess to be in his late teens, early twenties. He also wore the same color shirt as the older man, but his skin was over tanned.

"How's it going?" the younger guy asked.

"Not too bad," Cliff answered. "We saw you waving. No one stopping, huh?"

The men glanced at each other, and then back to Cliff, who stood on the bow of my skiff. The younger man spoke, "Yeah, we've waved to 'bout dozen boats so'far. No takers, I guess."

"What's seems to be the problem?" Cliff asked. "Engine trouble?"

The kid scratched his head. "Yeah, you guys wouldn't happen t'have a fifteen-amp fuse, would yah? The ignition fuse blew out and I lef'the spares in the truck, back at the ramp."

After hearing the problem these two were facing, I let go of the wheel. In the rear hatch I removed my toolbox that held mostly spare parts. Inside was the black pouch where I kept the small stuff; screws, a short coil of #14 gauge wire, and blade fuses—things I didn't need to get wet.

"I'm pretty sure I've got some in here." I sifted through the parts on my palm. "Here we go."

The younger man stepped to his bow, and to him I passed the fuse.

He held it to his eyes. "Oh, thanks! This could be exactly what w'need ... appreciate it."

"No problem," I replied. "Glad we could help."

He went right to work. "It's kinda hard t'get people t'stop and give a guy a hand when there's a big tourney goin' on."

"Yes ... it is," I replied. "Speaking of the tournament ... you guys in it?"

The kid was now bent over, head buried in the center console under the helm covered in a wired bird's nest. "Yeah, we're in her alright. Got a few nice ones to weigh-in, too! You guys?"

Cliff spoke first. "No, no, just out on a normal day of fishing."

The older gentleman didn't say so much as one word and sat crossed-legged on an old, rotted plank used for a front bench. His condition seemed rough, but relaxed; hands folded as if on heavy medication.

"Got her," the young guy called out. He rolled to his seat, reaching to where the ignition should have been, except there wasn't one. Bare-handed, he licked his fingertips and touched together two exposed wires, though he had done it a million times. After the visible flywheel began to spin, the engine started up and sounded strong.

"There she is," he said. The engine coughed and spit out plumes of two-stroke smoke.

"Man, you should get that fixed," I said. "That might be your problem."

"Yeah, been meanin' t'get to it, but since Dad…" He nodded to the elder. "Been sick, money's been kinda tight."

"Understandable," I said—then tried levity, "Hey, this old girl managed to produce two nice fish to weigh-in, though—still got some life left in her."

I'd noticed a seventeen-gallon baitwell was loosely bolted to the front deck, where two red shadows swam in tight circles. He said, "Yeah caught these two here in the same hole … right 'round the corner from Tur'le Bay."

Cliff agreed. "Nice. I'm Cliff, and this is my buddy, Shamus."

"Good to meet yah'two. This is m'dad, Pete, and I'm Randy." Pete uncrossed his hands and gently waved—a familiar motion, shaped by a lifetime of polite introductions.

"It's good to meet you two as well," I replied.

The kid moved behind the wheel. "I think we're gonna head on back and get these bulls weighed in and relax for a'few … maybe snag a beer."

"Sounds good," I replied. "You guys watch that chop. It's getting nasty out there."

"Will do. Thanks again."

I nodded, and the kid engaged the boat to idle. After clearing the mangroves, they reached plane, spreading a whitewash of wake.

After the boat was out of sight, Cliff said, "I hope they make it back."

****

We reached Cape Haze Peninsula fifteen minutes later, and clear from the cruising lane, I settled off plane and poled toward the mangroves then asked Cliff, "Hey, I was just wondering, how did you meet Mr. Northwood, Graham?"

Cliff was peeling back the tinfoil shell of an arugula wrapped turkey sandwich he had removed from the cooler. His answer included a mouthful. "Came into the deli about a month ago." He chewed and finished, "heard from another client that I do catering jobs."

"I see…"

Cliff continued, "I've only known him a month or so, and he seemed like a decent guy. Plus, he pays *really* well."

"Do you know what he did for a living? I mean, how he got rich?"

"Yah know, I'm not too sure. I think he ran some sort of consignment company, where he sells people's stuff for a cut of the price. Not just some rinky-dink local store. From what I heard around, it's a ginormous company."

I nodded.

"I've heard him talk about how he sells lots of boats, plus jet skis—things like that."

"Really?" My interest piqued. I let Cliff finish.

"Yeah, he's even talked about how some of his clients never collect their checks after he sells the items, so he keeps it. I mean the money."

"Kinda of a shady business practice…"

"Depends … if you don't pick up the check after he sells your stuff, after being notified, he's within his right to keep your shit."

I said, "How do you forget leaving something at a consignment shop?"

Cliff shrugged.

The sandwich was gone and as we sat, Cliff tied on a soft plastic lure and fired it fifty feet toward a limp mangrove branch.

As he tried casting, a high-speed tournament official—a spotter boat—raced by, identified from the snapping spotter flag inserted in the stern rod holder. I mumbled, "Even these guys think they own the place." Curious, I levered the boat in gear, and Cliff reeled up.

We sprang on plane, fell in behind the boat, following in its wake. We rounded Cape Haze Peninsula, rode the tight channel between the mangrove wall and the shallow flats.

We eased into Turtle Bay, idling through a short NO WAKE ZONE that, to everyone's credit, most boaters seemed to honor. The spotter boat, just ahead, fell off plane and swerved suddenly toward the mangroves. It didn't take long to see why. Two officials on the spotter boat were inspecting the gear of a tournament team.

"You see that?" I asked Cliff.

I shook my head. "Treble hooks."

The fishermen were using treble hooks to snag fish fleeing from a narrow creek adjacent to the channel. Snagging tournament fish was a violation of tournament rules, and also illegal. More importantly, if you get caught doing it, you were now known as a low life, bottom-dwelling maggot, who should be banished from the face of the Earth. It was safe to assume that these two were out of the tournament, and most likely banned for life.

After the water settled, a manatee surfaced ahead of the skiff.

The fat sea cow must have weighed close to a ton. Surfacing only its two big-holed, bowling ball-sized nostrils. Bold whiskers surrounded a snout. Manatees were harmless creatures, and if spotted, more times than not, would brandish violent body scarring, identifying its vicious encounters with humans. They're a protected species and even touching one in the wild might get you a hefty fine.

The sun rose fast, bringing with it a uptick in humidity. Before long, the sweat began to drip. The shoreline needed a scan for the suspects Brant and Co., so I did, in hopes of spotting the Pathfinder. Cliff didn't hesitate, took the binoculars, and did the same.

"Since you have the binoculars, you scan the west." I suggested. "I'll look to the east."

I started at the southern tip and scanned my way north but nothing. "Anything?" I asked.

"Yeah, there's plenty of action along the west side … not seeing the same Pathfinder though."

I free-eyed the shoreline. "East side is bunk." Then I scanned south toward the open harbor and wondered if Brant and his crew had stayed in the area—or had they turned south toward Pine Island Sound? Traveling southward could have its advantages for tournament fishermen. For one, there would be fewer teams fishing so far south. Also, the spotters would be less willing to follow them. Cliff and I couldn't travel those kinds of distances, due to the restraints of time.

I sighed. "I guess we wait."

****

In addition to offering semi-cover from the sun, our location provided a wide bearing, full panoramic view of the harbor. No one would sneak their boats past us.

While the push-pole pinned the skiff tight, paralleling us to the mangroves, Cliff went for his jerkbait rod and slung one out along the mangrove bushes. He twitched the stick methodically, darting the clear artificial bait, flitting it side-to-side a foot beneath the surface. I climbed up to the poling platform to scout. We were floating in four or five feet of emerald-green water, pressed against a mangrove barrier. Mullet bathed in casual tight-knit circles, and in the shallower areas, seagrass swayed alongside every gust of wind.

Cliff made multiple no-action casts.

"Nothing, huh?" I asked.

"Not a thing," he said.

"This spot used to produce." I dropped down from the platform and obtained a cold bottled water from the cooler.

Two wrapped tinfoil logs were inside a sealed Ziploc bag—both eight inches long and reflected the sunlight. Cliff brought us lunch that he no doubt prepared at *Gribbles* the previous night. I saw him eat an arugula wrap earlier, and I was excited for my chance. I peeled back the foil. Romaine lettuce kept it together, and rainbowing the insides were carrots, beets, red bell peppers, and I'm guessing zucchini. I was ready to eat. Aromatic blackened turkey hit my face, and hummus was the spread. I bit as Cliff watched for a reaction.

"Good?" he asked.

I chewed, crunching the leafy crust. "So far … delicious."

"It's a new recipe I've been trying out."

"Seems pretty simple," I pointed out. "Taste decent. I like the added hummus. Gives it a nice kick."

I sat back and let my stomach do what it did after a meal. A few boats out in the open flew from around mangrove corners. One dropped off plane and began to troll. I reached for the binoculars and peered.

Tournament teams were easy to spot. For one, each team must wear the same team across the shoulders of the shirts. In this case, it was a black, white-lettered Columbia shirt, and the name was too far away to read. Plus, they were what I call speed fishing.

The man on the bow ran the trolling motor and the other stood astern. Both fished repetitiously as they cast out lures. One guy was "walking the dog." The other slung a jerkbait equivalent to Cliff's. It was an expressed pace, and if they kept it up, they would be in our face in no time. I didn't mind or anything. The *Buff* cloaked our faces, leaving a low chance of identification unless they recognized my skiff, which stayed a possibility.

A primitive part of me sought to guard the fishing spot, block anyone from taking fish from it. It was a honey hole that produced large numbers of client-conducive fish when using the proper bait. A struggling charter captain like myself, finding a new honey hole that yielded fish in a habitual fashion was an essential gold mine, an untapped source of endless catches. When a spot was hot, its success was temporary. Fish move, and that was a fact.

Cliff began eating another sandwich, crunching up the ambiance.

The speed fishermen were gaining on us, which had the potential to expose crucial information if it displayed us catching fish, so I unhooked the push pole and snuck away from the mangroves. The wind found the skiff, and though taken by Mother Nature's hand, swept us further into the open flats.

The water wasn't deep, two feet at best. Visible bottom caught Cliff's attention as we hovered over sand hole after sand hole. He tossed a white jerkbait onto the sandy floor as we continued at the mercy of the wind. He began to retrieve, working the bait across the intended target. Using sharp flicks of the rod's tip, he took a crack at triggering a snook, or redfish or trout, waiting to ambush in the grass-filled shadows.

Cliff sighed. "Not even a boil."

"At least we tried."

Cliff followed my lead as I stepped to the wheel, and he reeled up his line. He hooked the lure on the eyelet saver above the corked handle and set the rod in the rod holder.

His tone sounded dejected. "So, you think we're gonna find Brant?"

Pausing for a second, I replied, "I'm not sure. It's counterproductive … just driving around at random." I gazed down the seven mile stretch of the West Wall, where hundreds of nooks and crannies could conceal traps or hidden pens, or even boats. "There's too much ground to cover and *not* enough time."

Chapter Six

I sat, and not to my surprise, the afternoon sea breeze had brought cooler winds from the Gulf to collide with warmer winds from the east, producing convective activity ripe for up-drafting winds and possibly dangerous thunderstorms. Crossing the harbor sprang to mind. My lightweight skiff was no stranger to the white-capped sea, but gunwales short as mine, getting swamped seemed guaranteed.

A few hours remained until the end of the tournament. And from our current stakeout location, returning to the Punta Gorda Boat Ramp where weigh-ins took place would take nearly forty-five-minutes.

I let the wind sweep us where it may momentarily, eventually setting the push pole deep in the sand—pinning us parallel along the West Wall's southern tip, against a fallen mangrove tree stump.

We lingered. Cliff continued casting lures into a deep trough. I broke away from the shiny stainless-steel steering wheel, opened the cooler, and pulled out a bag of sunflower seeds. After loading up my cheek like a chipmunk, I sat back in the captain's chair.

Hard wind then blew toward the open harbor and white caps swelled to three feet high. One mile out, a respectable-sized center console battered waves off its deep vee. The boat's trouble was a good sign of what our return trip might entail. The distant boat reminded me of why I was out—to catch Brant red-handed. If he and his crew had remained on our side of the harbor, it meant, on their return, they had to cross where we sat.

I spit a cracked-open sunflower seed into the water. "I think our best bet is to sit right here for a few minutes, then head back to weigh-ins."

"Whatever you want to do, brother," Cliff said—then flogged the stick, sending the lure out. "How nice would it be to catch a cobia right now?"

"Cobia?" I asked, intrigued.

"Yeah, big ol' cobia be nice right now."

"Yeah, toss him on the grill later," I added. "Delicious."

"I wouldn't mind biting into one right now."

"That would be something," I said. "When's the last time you caught a cobia?"

"A year ago."

One hour, and a full-eaten bag of sunflower seeds later, and no cobia, I glanced up at the burning sun, pulled the *Buff* off, and dunked it in the cooler. Ice-cold water shocked shivers down my spine after placing it back on.

I decided to join Cliff and cast a few, so I grabbed my Stradic 3000 strapped to a Red Bone and made a whopper toward a bank of mangroves lining the deep channel. Working the top water plug side to side, cold water droplets dripped from the *Buff* down my back and gave me a moment of reprieve. Powerful UV rays reflected off the water's rippled surface and into my sunglass-protected eyes.

Cliff set his rod down. "Seems like they're not biting at all today."

I let out a breath. "Over-fished."

Cliff, now deflated too, reached into the cooler where he found a bottled water.

I continued casting, and in the distance, kept a close eye on the passing boaters. A surface boil from the corner of my eye triggered an instinctual fast-cast toward it. At first, it looked like a school of mullet, their tails flicking above the surface in tight formation—until a sudden commotion erupted beneath them, scattering the fish into a frenzied burst of silver and spray.

"Every mullet for itself," I muttered, but kept working the top water lure. "I hope you're watching this," I said to Cliff, as he gulped water.

As though a pause in time, a mouth the size of a five-gallon bucket engulfed the Zara Spook. "Did you see that?" I shouted.

"No, I missed it. Big snook?"

"Oh, no … this is *no* snook, Cliff."

I leaned forward, bowing the rod toward the fish, bracing to set the hook, then yoked, arching the rod, tightening the braided twenty-pound line. The fish felt the abnormality and skyrocketed from the water, folded in half, and sent pounding percussions into my chest.

"Poon!" belted Cliff.

The fish zinged line off the small, 3000 series Stradic. I cupped the spool, frantic to slow the fish. Such power ripped good line, yard after yard, off the tiny reel.

I clamped my teeth together. "Feels like fighting a dump truck!"

The fish darted toward the mangroves—one hundred yards out.

Cliff rushed next to me. "Where's he at?"

I labored out the words, "He's way out, over there. Ahead of the dead branch on the other side of the oyster bed. See 'em?" I was desperate to gain line into the reel and continued cranking but was only given the fast click of drag.

The line tightened, then it sliced to the surface, which meant the fish was poised to launch again. Another dramatic aerial display happened, but before I could prepare, a slow-motion bust through the reflective water, then a snapping head shake, and a splash down was all it took. Immediately, I knew I had lost it.

Cliff knew the answer. "He break off?"

I sliced the rod tip through the water, frustrated and deflated. "Yup."

Before Cliff and I had a chance to relive the exciting moment, a towered Pathfinder screamed around the corner, creating high wake rolling into my skiff, listing us off balance. There was no mistaking the barreling boat's phosphorous green hull. The tower-perched captain wore a red visor; long blond hair flopped out from under it. There was no confusion this time. This was our boat.

"I think that was him!" Cliff said.

"That was definitely him." I rushed around, reeling up line. "We need to get going now. I won't lose him again." I loaded the push pole into the clips and cranked the engine, hammering down the throttle, launching the skiff hard, rocketing the bow vertically toward the semi-cloudy blue sky.

After the bow came down, we settled on plane, following in the Pathfinder's wake. Boy did Brant's boat move fast. The two-stroke scent was strong as we swept through the fuel-saturated plumes, and facing ahead, it was clear in a matter of minutes, they had gained a mile on us.

Cliff took the binoculars and set them to his eyes. He half-turned and spoke above the engine: "I bet they're headed for weigh-ins."

"I think you're right," I said. "And by the speed they're running, I'd say they're in some sort of hurry— but then again, you never know. Guys like that haul ass … just to haul ass."

My sixty-horsepower engine maxed at six thousand RPMs as we cruised a steady thirty miles per hour. Our heading pressed the wind on our backs, squeezing out an extra mile an hour.

Ahead, I tapped Cliff on the shoulder. "What time are weigh-ins exactly?"

The binoculars hung around his neck. He spoke from the corner of his mouth: "I think they're at three."

"If the weigh-ins were held at three p.m., we gotta catch these guys doing something stupid before returning to the dock."

Moving along, far fewer fishermen remained along the West Wall than on the way out. If teams had caught and secured their allotted fish for the tournament, there was no reason to keep fishing and risk a fish kill.

A small silhouette of Brant's boat was just a blip— we'd trailed the boat midway down the West Wall. If Brant was indeed headed to weigh-ins at the Punta Gorda Boat Ramp, he would have changed course and fixed east, cutting across the harbor, but he had continued north. It was possible, though, Brant and his crew had come up empty, and arriving skunked at weigh-ins, his frustration had manifested as speed.

I continued scanning the shoreline but then decided on taking a chance, so I changed course myself, aiming for weigh-ins.

Cliff then stood and pointed ahead. "They stopped," he said, waving me to slow.

I levered the skiff to idle speed and stood.

Cliff handed me the binoculars, and said. "They've slowed, bro, and for whatever reasons, made a turn portside, to the mangroves."

"There's a decent-sized creek where they've stopped."

"Oyster Creek!"

The twenty-two-foot boat idled into the creek; its engine trimmed up.

"Let's inch our way up," I said. "See what's going on..."

Cliff sat back and became comfortable. "Sounds good to me."

I recognized the creek they entered. I'd fished Oyster Creek many times. At thirty feet across, it was mid-sized and zig-zagged quite a way into the bush. Long ago, at a time of bountiful catches, it proved to be an excellent charter spot for clients, but over time it had been utterly fished out.

Not one boat was fishing the initial deep channel running portside along the mangroves. I used caution approaching the mouth. Brant and his men had pushed their way up and around the first watery dogleg, which meant Cliff and I had a chance to tail.

"You want to just pole us in?" Cliff suggested. "Be quieter." He pulled down his *Buff*, exposing his lips.

"I think that's the smartest thing to do. At this point, even if he spots us, he won't be able to tell who we are."

I gripped the push pole and climbed up to the poling platform, remembering that the creek spread to a small, secluded lake, close to the size of my own basin. A high-flying bird looking down would see the shape of a sperm, tail illustrating the entrance, and at what would be the sperm's eyes, a shallow, nasty shoal. Brant and his crew might indeed make a last-stitch effort to bag a fish.

I kept a vigilant eye ahead, poling us around the first bend. We'd come this far so spooking Brant, or his first mate, would be disastrous.

Rounding the second bend in caution, Cliff stood on the bow and readied for anything.

"What do you see?" I asked.

"Nothing yet," Cliff whispered.

In the creek, I knew about three total switchbacks, or bends, leading to the open lake—we'd already passed two.

Through the thick greenery, the tropical mangroves reminded me of why Charlotte Harbor was so special, and why protecting it was crucial. The circuitous estuaries were a vital breeding ground for all sorts of marine life. On either side of the skiff, big mangrove bushes mixed in abundance among the gray swamp marl edging the bank; the tide dripped continually off the red-brown bush roots and trickled down the oysters into the water. The soft slap of water tapped the bow as I pushed along.

In an instant, halfway rounding the final bend before the small lake, Cliff waved. "What? You see something?" I whispered.

"Looks like they're floating around the shoal—not sure what they're doing though."

I received the binoculars from Cliff and handed him the push pole. Brant and Co. were floating idle, not casting bait or any kind of fishing. Brant pointed from up in the tower, aiming a finger ahead of the bow.

The other team member, who was wearing the cobalt team shirt, stood at the bow in a search pose.

"What are they doing?" Cliff asked.

"Pointing at something they've found."

"Oh…?"

"Yeah, now they've retrieved a rope, and the short dude is pulling it in like a crab pot."

"Crabs?"

Still peering through the binoculars, I added, "You better get out your phone and start recording. It ain't no crab pot."

Chapter Seven

After a raw taste of Mother Nature's power, we glided into the Punta Gorda Boat Ramp basin. Battered and wet, the chop had reached nearly five-foot. I had to slow our speed, returning most of the trip on a half-plane, but not before smashing my nose on the steering wheel, which then bled. I had made good use of the *Buff* to soak up blood.

Brant and his sidekick had arrived far ahead.

Cliff stood and wrenched his shoulder, then rubbed his hands. The whole trip, he had clamped the bow rope for support. "That was one of the roughest rides I've ever been on. Remember the ceiling rope we'd climb in high school?"

"Yup."

"That's what I'm feeling right now."

I smiled. "You're welcome."

"You might want to check the hull for stress cracks."

"Nah, she's fine…" I petted the steering wheel, "…wants to go back across."

Cliff observed the blood. "How's your nose?"

I pulled the *Buff* down using my fingertips. The blotches of red were turning dark, drying toward brown, but blended into the camouflage print. "I'll live."

****

We kept idling, passing boat after docked boat. Shiny, expensive, custom skiffs lined in rows, packed like cattle. It was an impressive display, notable to even the average boater. It seemed similar as finding a parking spot at a crowded sporting event. All slips had been taken.

Cliff held his phone. "What should we do with the pictures and video, since you ain't no rat?" He smiled.

I thought about it briefly. "I'd like to find a movie theater-size screen and play it for the entire crowd, exposing the two slime-balls, but that's probably not an option."

"That would be so wrong and so right at the same time. But if you're not going to turn them in, then what?"

"Good question. I'll have to think of a way to resolve this another way."

He leaned in. "Which is…?"

"No idea."

Cliff focused on finding an empty dock cleat, pointing at a splintered pine plank. "One loose … right there."

The slip was vacant for obvious reasons.

"Kinda shallow," I said.

"Might be the only spot open, though."

"It'll have to do," I said—then geared the engine and targeted the open cleat attached to the dock piling. The piling had three feet of exposed crustaceans adhering like cement to areas that normally remain underwater. Below that: six inches of water. As we approached the dock, distant cheers echoed to us.

"Did you hear that?" I asked.

Cliff held the bow rope, ready to receive the dock piling. "Sounds like they're weighing in fish already."

According to my watch, the three o'clock margin had passed.

Cliff tied off the skiff, and I heaved onto the dock while gripping a pylon cleat and followed Cliff a short ten feet to the end of the wooden dock, where the concrete walkway began.

The tournament weigh-ins were held in an adjacent parking lot past an old bait shop overlooking The Peace River. A metal stage was erected where teams and their families could watch the proceedings. Specific weigh-in times weren't given to the teams, but the sooner the fish was weighed and handed to the release boat, the better. Most teams in the tournament wouldn't weigh-in a single fish—others might weigh in only one fish, but the pageantry of the weigh-ins drew in hefty crowds.

As we strolled near the bait shop, and before entering the main crowd, groups of righteous protesters lingered, positioned harmlessly at the entrance to the stage while an irritated-looking rent-acop grudgingly watched. As people rushed by them, they spouted off things like: "DO YOU KNOW WHAT YOU'RE DOING TO THE PLANET'S RESOURCES?" And "FISH HAVE RIGHTS!" Another said, SAVE HORSE CREEK. They harassed people who dared to get close. One distinctive protester, who appeared to be the leader, shouted the most while the others followed his lead. One of them, a young girl, held a sign that read: TOURNAMENTS KILL! DEPLETION IS REAL! That one I agreed with.

"See those guys?" Cliff asked.

"Yes, same ones every time. I wish there were more of them."

We continued, passing rows of tawdry dealer tents selling everything from fishing reels to boat engines. A few people mingled, holding brochures as a salesman pointed out important details.

"Decent turnout," I said.

"Where do you want to search first?" Cliff asked.

"I have no idea, but it shouldn't be difficult to find them. Just follow the stench of douche."

Cliff laughed.

The corner of the stage held a tournament poster listing prizes and giveaways that hung from an outward beam with $25,000 stenciled banner-styled arched across the top. Below that, centered, pictured a brand new, fully-loaded Hewes flats boat—gorgeous machine.

Cliff's eyes swept the poster, asked, "Think they already weighed in?"

"Let's go check the leaderboard."

We strolled the short walk to the opposite corner of the stage, where hung a large digital leaderboard. I scrolled through the lists.

"You see that?" Cliff said. "It's listed by team names."

I scanned the crowd. "That's going to make things interesting."

"Team *Second Chance* is in the lead," Cliff noted.

Soon as Cliff finished his words, a team appeared on stage presenting two hardy-sized redfish.

"Those don't look too bad," my friend said. The fish were brought alongside two participants and swam in a clear bag holding blue-dyed, highly oxygenated water. The team weighing their catch appeared to be a sponsored, professional team—big-patched name brands plastered across their shirts.

After the catch had been weighed, both men were handed a slippery fish, then posed for pictures. People in the crowd reacted colorfully, swinging up cameras for photos—some recorded video.

Cliff said, "Those two pigs might give them a chance."

At first glance, only a few teams had weighed in their fish, so we had plenty of time to loiter. Team after team plopped their redfish onto the scale. After each team, it seemed the crowd thickened. Multiple clusters of participants socialized and mingled, discussing their favorite techniques or "never fail" lures.

The high sun meant very little shade to be had, so I strolled to the beer tent and stumbled upon a small patch of shaded solitude. On the way, people who knew Cliff held him up repeatedly.

The shade was nice, and I again scanned the crowd, searching for Brant. Neither he nor his friend were anywhere in sight. After a few cool minutes under shade, Cliff arrived.

"Any sign of them?" he asked.

"Nope." I panned out to the crowd. "I know they're around here somewhere."

A few idle minutes ticked away, then Cliff slapped my shoulder. "Hey, look!" He pointed toward the stage.

The first thing I noticed on stage was the top of Brant's head. Hair like a yellow mop, tucked under a red faded visor.

"Should we get closer?" Cliff asked.

"Maybe a little bit closer. I still don't want them seeing us."

Even though I still had the *Buff*, I decided wearing it while walking through the crowd might seem suspicious.

We found a hidden corner of the stage, behind a Port-A-Jon, and spied. An official took Brant's and Co. fish from the clear carrying bag and laid them on a stainless-steel scale.

The announcer ceremoniously pumped up the crowd. "Come on, folks … is it gonna be enough to take the lead? Will team *Shallow Life* win the whole thing?"

Cliff observed what I was thinking. "Well, now we know what their team's name is."

"Name fits." My blood boiled while watching the two cheaters on stage, knowing that those redfish weren't legit. The beginnings of a malevolent grin began developing on Brant's face. The shorter, and bulkier of the two, Brant's friend, didn't seem as excited. Maybe he had a conscience.

Cliff's eyes widened. "They're going need at least seventeen pounds, nine ounces to take the lead."

"No way can they beat that," I replied from the corner of my mouth. "That's a lot of fish."

The announcer's delay in revealing the accumulated weight sold anticipation to the crowd. And by their traits, it was working. After a long and unnecessary amount of buildup, the leaderboard flashed the combined weight of the fish. It read: seventeen pounds, eleven ounces.

The crowd erupted in cheers. Brant and his buddy shook congratulatory hands and then bro-hugged. The announcer's hand was splayed on Brant's shoulders as he shook each man's hand. A tournament official commandeered their fish, splashing them back into the blue bag, whisking them away as if they were celebrities.

Cliff showed me a concern-lined expression. He knew I wouldn't react lightly to it. "I can't believe it," I muttered. "They won."

The blood pulsing through my veins felt like battery acid. My gut reaction was strong. "That's it," I said. "I can't let them get away. I'm showing them the photos and video footage and putting an end to this." I made off toward the stage, where teams exited after weighing in. Cliff followed.

"What are you gonna do to them?" he asked.

I didn't answer but stomped toward Brant in a furious rage. But it was short-lived because standing twenty feet from the cheater, I froze in shock. Standing at the end of the steps heading off the stage was Dr. Clara Hayes. She wore a blue pair of woman's board shorts and a flamingo-colored fishing shirt; hair in a bun tucked under a mesh trucker's hat. She appeared to be waiting for someone—and that someone was Brant.

Chapter Eight

Standing in shock, I managed a weak step, ducking behind a small huddle of people, wishing Dr. Clara hadn't seen me. I then broke into a stride in the opposite direction.

Cliff paced fast behind me. "What's the matter?" he asked. "There they are, right there." He pointed two fingers.

"I know, I know. Did you see the brunette standing at the base of the stairs?"

We stopped and Cliff leaned, peering over a man's shoulder. "Yeah, in the pink shirt?"

I nodded intently. "Yeah, that's the one."

"What about her?"

"Do you see who she's with?"

Cliff looked again. "Oh … well, since she just gave Brant a hug, I'd say *him*. What's the big deal, brother? Let's go expose his ass!"

"I know her. That's Scupper's veterinarian."

Cliff was pulling me ahead. "What's that got to do with anything?"

"I'd rather not confront Brant with her present."

Cliff cracked a smile. "I see what's goin' on here... What's the plan, then?"

"I'm not sure." I started back to the shady patch under the beer trailer awning. "Yeah, we dated, Dr. Clara and I, for a few months, on and off," I explained to Cliff as we walked. "I just wasn't expecting to see her here, and especially not with Brant. Don't you remember her?"

Cliff scanned the stage. "Yeah, I remember her now. From the looks of it, I'd say *they're* dating now."

"Sure does," I replied. "I just wonder what she sees in him … I mean, *really?*"

"Money," Cliff answered wryly.

I scoffed. "She's a veterinarian, so she's not hurting for money, by any means."

"I'm not saying that she's dating him for his money, brother. I'm saying that she's dating him because *he* has his *own* money."

"I see your point." Hearing those words didn't comfort me at all. "Are you saying that maybe the reason we had such a tough time was because I was broke most of the time?"

Cliff attempted to backpedal. "Whoa … I'm not sayin' that. I mean, maybe she just wanted a change. Yah know how women are…"

My mind was blown. "But this guy, really?"

"You seem upset. Why?"

"I mean, c'mon … that guy?" I pointed, then turned to Cliff. His smirk told me everything—my feelings were written all over my face.

"You're not jealous, are you?"

There wasn't anything I could say, it was obvious.

I turned back to the mission, back to the stage where Brant's victory gloat continued while Graham Northwood stood next to him, also appearing congratulatory, and then a short woman, wearing an event staff shirt holding a clipboard, ambled up to the small group and spoke to the winners, gathering info. The men stood for a few more minutes, rejoicing. Graham then shook both men's hands, nodded to the woman, and walked off.

The woman ushered Brant and his friend through the crowd and into a white tent. As the white door flap opened, I glimpsed another man inside. It appeared to be the same grumpy, bushy-browed man from Graham's party. Something didn't add up. My gut-reaction surfaced, and I stomped forward in monstrous fume. "Screw this. I'm gonna go show them what we've got."

"Nice!" replied Cliff.

As I stepped again, my phone chimed.

It was a text message from Sara. *I'm at the house and Scupper is missing!*

"Damn," I said.

"What's the matter?" asked Cliff.

I began to call Sara, faced Cliff, and said, "Scupper got out."

"Hello, Shamus?" Sara asked on the phone.

"Yes, it's me. What going on?"

"Oh, thank God. I came to let Scuppers out and she's not here. I can't find her." Sara spoke with concern, then her tone rose to a shriek. "I don't know where she is, Shamus!"

I told her to calm down, she had probably gotten loose.

"You still fishing or whatever?"

I wasn't sure the time had come to include her with our discovery. "Not exactly."

"Not exactly?"

"We're at the weigh-ins," I said. "Leaving now."

"Okay, hurry!"

"Give me about thirty minutes."

I hung up the phone. "We've got to go."

"Go?" he asked, confused. "Where?"

"Scupper is missing, and Sara's losing it."

"Where'd she go?"

"Not sure. Sara's at the house now."

I motioned toward the dock where my skiff lay.

Cliff stopped mid-stride. "Hey, I think I might stay. Yah know … little recon, see where these guys go."

"You don't mind?" I asked.

"No, not at all, brother. There's still plenty of time left here. People ain't gonna leave right away. I'll just hang and feel things out, make a few connections— network."

Out towards the harbor, a bundle of busy winds began to press on the waves, riling them into rolls of fierce traveling humps of water.

I turned back to Cliff. "You may have to wait here for a couple hours, because if you take a look out there…" I pointed harborside. "The winds are charged up, blowing like a madman."

Cliff said, "I don't mind." I heard the sincerity in his voice. "Really, it's fine."

"Sounds like a plan." I nodded and stepped away. "I'll call you when I'm leaving the house so keep your ears on. Thirty minutes."

Cliff twisted an imaginary knob near his ear. "Gotcha."

I began snaking through the crowd, heading for the docks. As I left the crowd at the entrance, the protesters were still holding their ground. If they had a donation jar, I might have donated. They were no doubt barred from entering. Normally they would have been granted full access, but an underhanded event change a few years ago moved the weigh-ins onto private property. Entering might get a trespassing charge slapped on them.

I managed three steps from the concrete path leading to the lip of the wooden-planked dock when I glanced up, and at that exact moment he saw me. Immediately, I wished I had taken a different route.

"Hey! Shamus, right?" Randy asked—the same Randy I had given fuses to earlier in the day.

"Hey," I said in an obviously distant tone.

The kid had smooth, hairless arms, tanned deep. His head was shaved thin under a camouflage visor. His right hand held a filled cup of foam-topped beer. Motioning for a handshake, he reached the other one out. "Hey, I wanted t'thank you again. You really helped out me and my dad."

I implied again in the direction I was walking, passing the hint along. "Really, it was no big deal. Glad we could help."

He sensed my haste but paid no mind to it. "Yeah, Dad … he's real sick … liver failure. He's waiting awn a transplant."

Being caught off guard, I blurted, "Oh, sucks." I immediately regretted it, but I *was* needed somewhere else.

He went on, "My dad? He a tough old geezer, and this tournament? Kinda bucket list thing." The kid laid his hand on my shoulder to guide me. "C'mon, friend, let m'buy yah a beer?" His breath smelled worse than a dog's fart.

I bent back and removed his hand. "I really appreciate it, maybe another time."

"Oh … just one … c'mon." The more this guy talked, the more he made sense. "What's the harm?"

"Really, I do appreciate it, but I'm in kind of a hurry."

"Okay, okay." He relented, and the beer came close to spilling as he swung out. "Here take mine, then."

The full, ice-cold beer still dripped condensation as frothy foam overflowed. "Oh, what the hell." I accepted the beer—to make up for the "sucks" comment. "Thanks."

His eyes slanted. "You still gotta let me repay you somehow."

I raised the cup. "The beer is plenty, really."

"No, no. Out of dozens of boaters, you and your friend were the *only* ones who made time to t'help us."

I thought for a second. "Well … let me get your number and I'll call you when I think of something."

"Deal!" he said.

I loaded his number into my phone's memory.

On a good note, my skiff remained where I had left her, sitting pretty on a motionless canvas of water. I untied the dock line and pushed off. The tide had risen a few inches, granting me a touch of freedom to tilt the engine down and idle off. As I rounded the last set of docks before the end of an IDLE ZONE, the view of the crowd improved, and its increase in size was clearly visible. I mumbled, "It seems most teams had lingered around to watch the weigh-in ceremony."

I idled through the channel markers under the Punta Gorda Bridge and faced the wind head-on. Intimidating whitecaps blanketed the harbor like a snow-dusted lake. The scene resembled an old seascape painting, an artistic high-sea emphasis: black waves, small white tips at the crest; and far-off winds appeared like thick clouds of haze. The sun was high, and its rays bent from the power of the wind. I gulped the beer, in hopes of keeping the spillage to a minimum.

Nearly five minutes in, I was getting battered silly, so I headed near the Colony Point Condos, and to my surprise, the tournament's release boat sat west of the condos along the shallow bar. "Hmmm…" I mumbled. The boat appeared to have just arrived and set adrift. One man was bent over, hands inside a large surface-mounted oval bait tank, reaching, netting the swimming fish.

There were a few curious onlookers nearby, casting out lines. After the traumatic events that the fish had just been through, a bite seemed unlikely.

The boats drifted closer like gators prowling on a meal. Voices rose and fell across the water, their words distant and indistinct. A release boat occupant held up a hand, signaling to the approaching boats to hold a moment.

I became interested.

The onlooking boater geared his motor, and a minute later they were damn near lashed together.

"What is going on?" I muttered.

It was then, things got weird. The assumed captain of the release boat flung a hearty-sized stud of a redfish into the arms of the eager onlooker. Slippery when wet, the man who received the precious redfish dropped it onto his deck. He scrambled to pin it down, and after recovering, torpedoed it headfirst into his recessed stern live well.

"Unbelievable."

Another onlooker inched near, he too perked like a prairie dog, impatient for a handout.

Another, and then another, the release boat captain flung one fish into the harbor, one to the mendicant onlookers.

I raised my arms to them in disbelief. The lowlife boaters paid no mind to me and approached as though vultures waiting their turn on an African carcass. Upset, I sped off as one of them began to moon me.

****

Rounding the mangrove point at Ponce de Leon Park, the rolling, white-capped waves turned against me, slamming broadside into the skiff, jolting me off my line. I turned, now into the wind, pressing into the palpable gusts as though every sharp burst might give rise to the bow—flipping me into the harbor.

I clenched the stainless-steel, light-reflecting wheel and routed the boat to the east, a hundred or so yards toward the mangroves. I was desperate to find consistency to the chop, which at a height of three or four feet, in a lightweight skiff, bounced me around like a ping-pong ball.

An iconic soaring water tower came into view rounding Whore House Point. The tide along the mangroves was at a moderate, manageable height of less than a foot, and passing Poacher's Cut, I found reasonable shelter from the wind.

A flock of high-souring pelicans circled above, using the wind, lifting them, scoping for the right flash through the murky chop.

The remainder of the trip was uneventful, and with little-to-no bruising, I arrived unharmed at the mouth of my basin. As I idled along, Spinner was exhibiting bizarre behavior. It appeared to be swimming in circles, sometimes stopping to a bob position, submerging— and then repeating.

The dolphin's peculiar behavior piqued my interest, and approaching cautiously, I understood the inspiration behind the mammal's activity. Scupper was swimming in the water with it, seemingly in a playful manner, doggie-paddling for a few seconds, and then Spinner would swim underneath, lifting the pup onto its body above the dorsal fin. Scupper seemed to tease, nipping at Spinner's fin. It was quite an amazing pairing that I never had expected.

On the approach, Spinner abandoned Scupper, leaving her to swim to the ramp solo. Spinner then surfaced next to the skiff and let out a *poooeeesh* of air.

I drank the last remaining gulp of my foamy reward, bumped the houseboat, and tied off the skiff. Scupper had nearly swam to the boat ramp.

I deboarded, swept past the sea grape tree toward the boat ramp and called to Scupper. She saw me, barked, and doggie-paddled to the ramp—tongue hanging out to one side. Once on solid ground, her head twisted, transmitting movement all the way to the tip of her tail, drying herself off.

"Here, girl."

She trotted out from the boat ramp twitching, twisting, and leaping.

I knelt. "Where have you been?"

She jumped in my lap.

"Good girl."

Sara was jogging down to the path between the tall grass leading to the garage. She noticed us, paused, and placed her hands on her hips, mouth open, staring directed at Scupper.

"Where was she?" she asked.

"You're never going to believe it," I said, shaking my head.

Scupper trotted up and weaved between Sara's long legs. Sara leaned down and scratched the pup's head. "Oh, Scupper … you're all wet, jeez." She then wiped the wet film from her inside thigh, turned to me. "So, where was she, Shamus?"

"Swimming with Spinner."

"Excuse me?" she asked suspiciously.

"Yup. She was out in the basin." I pointed. "Swimming with the dolphin."

"Was she really?" Sara scratched a rib on Scupper. "What were you doing out there?" she said to the dog. "Pretty girl … swimming with Spinner … how cute. Did you make a friend?"

"Yup. Spinner was swimming right alongside her as Scupper did the 'ol doggie-paddle. Funny, every couple of seconds the dolphin submerged, then lifted her up from underneath. Simply incredible…"

"Wow," Sara responded. "I've never heard of such a thing. Have you?"

"Not of a dog and dolphin I haven't, but different types of animals make friends all the time. Ever been on a farm?"

She faced the basin. "Yes, but how did she get out there?"

"I think she just walked down the ramp and jumped in—simple. Come to think about it, it's kind of convenient for her." Now, as if impertinent, I said, "I see no harm letting her swim. The dolphin seems harmless enough."

Sara brought her arms to her shifting hips. "You can't be serious?"

"I'm quite serious. What could possibly go wrong?" Soon as my lips finished the last word, I knew it was dumb to ask.

"*What* could possibly go *wrong?*" she exclaimed. "She could *drown,* for one thing."

"Yes, you're right. That is a real possibility."

"Well?"

"Well, what?" I asked.

She respired, seemed to lasso her tone. "What if the dolphin gets aggressive and attacks her?"

"I really doubt that would happen. That dolphin has been nothing but nice and welcoming towards *me.*" A smile broke character. "I'm not sure there's any instances of dolphins attacking dogs."

"I'm not going to argue anymore," she said resolutely. "If that dolphin hurts her, it's on you."

I wrapped my arm around Sara and pulled her close. "Don't worry. Scupper survived wandering the neighborhood, and for all we know the whole town for months before I found her, so I think she'll be fine."

Sara pressed against my chest, and our tense friction melted away. Her chin raised for a kiss like a baby bird stretches for food. "How did it go? I mean out on the water?" Her expression turned concerning. "What happened to your *Buff*? Is that blood?"

"Yeah, smashed my nose on the steering wheel. No biggie."

She reached for my nose. "Oh, Shamus. Are you sure you're okay?"

"Yes, I'm fine."

She helped me along. "So, the tournament…?"

"It went just as planned."

"Really? Didn't you go with Cliff?"

"Yes, he stayed at the weigh-ins—keeping an eye on Brant."

She swung away her head. "You left him there? You know his truck is still parked in the driveway, right?"

"Yes. He offered to stay while I came to check on Scupper." Scupper was now trying hard to wedge herself between us. "You told me to hurry…"

"I know." She blew a strand of hair from her eye. "I was just afraid. I didn't know where she went, is all."

I said to comfort, "You did the right thing—calling me."

"The last place I'd expect her to be is in the dang water." Her voice now rose: "Swimming with a dolphin … jeez!" She stepped, showing off her loose-fitting shorts and tie-dyed shirt.

I pointed toward the basin. "Hey, I'm not saying you should have looked there. That's one sly pup."

Sara gazed toward a tilted sable palm. "Maybe we should tie her up—"

My face formed a serious grin as I swiped my hand through the air. "No way."

Her eyelids fluttered, enticing me to take a chance and explain. "Why not? It would make me feel *much* better."

"No way—never going to happen. She'll be fine, I promise."

We walked up to the house; Scupper led.

I opened the lanai screen door and Sara ducked under my arm. Scupper showed no interest in joining us. Now that the storm had begun to dissipate, she headed sluggishly to a sunny spot feet from the front door, rotated in two tight circles, and plopped down. Lethargic, no doubt.

Inside, I opened a room temperature bottle of water and guzzled it halfway empty.

"Thirsty?" Sara asked.

"Very," I replied, then asked, "Are you sure Brant didn't say anything else at the party? About his plans?"

She didn't bother to look my way. "Still on that, are we?"

"I could tell he was into you. I mean, he basically gawked at you while we were talking to Graham."

Sara stood at the kitchen counter sifting through her purse. "Okay, listen up, buddy." She used her eyes, held me. "He called *me* over when I was walking to

Cliff's van. All he said was that he really enjoyed the dinner, and that was it, okay?"

I did, in fact, believe her. Hearing the sincerity in her voice, I decided to let it go. "How did shopping go with your sister?"

"You mean my mother?" she corrected. "It was *for* my sister's wedding."

"Yeah," I nodded in recollection. "How did it go?"

"It was okay. We went to the Sarasota Outlet Mall."

I shook my head, showing mild interest. "Good, good."

"You couldn't care less."

"Not true…"

She smiled. "I've learned your ways well in these last several months, Shamus. You're distracted. What's on your mind? Did you find some dirt on Brant and those guys?"

"Yeah, we did … and it's kinda a big deal."

"Really?" She slid closer—disposed to absorb— asked, "What did you find?"

"Oh, that reminds me," I shifted toward the door. "I've got to go pick up Cliff. I have to go."

"Wait!" she said. "You find anything? That's the reason you went out today, right?"

"For the most part, yes," I said heading for the door. "…and yes, we *did* find something."

She followed me to the front door. "What did you find, Shamus?"

"I'll explain later. It's still preliminary, and right now I don't want to rush into anything. Cool?" That was partly true.

She shrugged sadly. "Oh—okay."

I wanted to confide, explain what Cliff and I had found, but the timing wasn't right for her to know. Danger wasn't my main concern with Brant and his partner. I felt it was better to see it to the end before playing her the footage. I could tell she felt left out, but did I trust her? Maybe a part of me thought she might be in on it. But why?

I shook my head. *You're being crazy,* I thought. "Trust me," I said to her, and then gripped the door handle. "I'll tell you everything later."

Through the threshold, on the way to my truck, I asked, "Oh, and can you lock up when you leave?" I climbed into the truck that was parked next to Cliff's Chevy, started it, and began reversing. Sara stood behind the shaded screen door, folding her arms. I hit the brakes, skidding on the gravel. I leaned out the window. "One more thing? Can you lay some food out for Scupper? Thanks!" In an instant, I bolted from the driveway, destination: downtown Punta Gorda.

Chapter Nine

After I'd parked the Toyota in the Punta Gorda Boat Ramp parking lot, I loitered at the loading dock parallel to the ramp and sent Cliff a text: I'm back. Where are you?

I then strolled toward the crowd, searching for Cliff. After five minutes of moseying, I reached one of the dealer tents. My phone beeped. A reply text from Cliff: tent beer.

The crowd had thinned, and when I arrived at the tent, Cliff was speaking to a fellow guide, Johnny Potts. One of Cliff's superpowers was that he knew more people in town than a fifty-cent whore.

Cliff held a fresh beer. "Shaaamus!"

I smiled at Cliff's belligerence. "I see you've been staying occupied."

"Just had a couple, brother."

I switched focus to Johnny Potts as Cliff introduced us. "You remember Johnny, right?" We shook hands, and Johnny flashed a haughty smile that revealed a front tooth so lifeless it looked one breath away from hitting the dirt. His arms were skinny, like pipes, and he was dressed in bright green fishing slacks and a thin, white polyester shirt covered his deeply tanned body. Along with the *Buff*, a straw hat sat atop his head. His beard was spotty, and difficult to tell where it ended and his chest began. Although I knew of Johnny Potts, and other professional guides, we didn't normally socialize, but sharing technical banter at these events was harmless. I gave Johnny the benefit of the doubt because I trusted Cliff's judgment in character.

"How's the bite been?" Johnny asked me.

"Can't complain."

Cliff burped, spoke with a slight slur, "Johnny here was tellin' me that they've been catching *monster* snook in the deep holes back in Bull Bay—cut bait. Oversized ones, too."

"Oh, yeah?" I projected the least amount of interest without sounding cheeky.

"Yeah, been catching 'em on cut ladyfish," Johnny added, chin up, seemed expecting an effervescent response.

During a recent scouting trip, I spotted a school of torpedo-sized snook lounging in Bull Bay, stretching forty inches apiece. But I felt no need to share this info. "Cool, cool," I replied—then asked Johnny, "Staying busy?"

"Oh, yeah, sure am," he answered. "Booked solid through August. About half of them doubles."

Cliff drank a slug of beer and belched. "I was tellin' Johnny that he should charge double when chartering these tournaments, man." Cliff was always thinking business, even buzzed.

Other charter guys knew I offered cut-rate trips, underpricing nearly everyone else. But none of them were aware I operated without a Merchant Mariner license.

I asked probed Jonny for info. "Did you charter this one?"

"Sure did—but caught only one little rat red," Johnny boasted. "About the only one I seen all day, which is kinda strange."

"Is that right?" I said, unimpressed.

"Yep. The little guy sat in a turtle grass-filled sand hole back in Bull Bay. Had a client spot cast him from about fifty-foot away. Took him about ten dang casts to hook it, though. Hard to believe some of these other guys have such gorgeous fish to weigh-in—especially the leaders, guys on top. I mean, where do they get them? Must be luck…"

I eyed Cliff.

"Makes a man wonder," Johnny said.

I glanced out at the crowd, which had faded to around fifty people, and had no sign of Brant or his sidekick. Cliff and Jonny began to chat, discussing the secrets of spot casting, and so I suspected Cliff had indeed fallen off mission, miss-cueing Brant from his sights. I had to silence him to not reveal any belligerent mission information. I didn't interrupt the chatter but waited for an opening. "You ready?" I said to insinuate haste, but more to separate the two and learn of Cliff's findings.

"Okay—nice seeing you," Cliff said to Johnny.

As they shook hands, I yoked Cliff's arm, and we paced away.

Johnny called to me, "Don't be a stranger, Shamus."

After a hundred feet, I said to Cliff, "I didn't see Brant and his friends anywhere. I thought you were keeping an eye on them?"

"Brother," Cliff replied in a tranquil, calming voice. "Don't freak out, I've got it covered."

"Covered?" I asked.

"Yes, covered."

"Then what is it?" I asked.

"After the weigh-ins, I followed Brant and his buddy to a sponsor tent. The one selling Penn Battle fishing reels. Oh, by the way, they have a kiiii-ller deal on a 4000 series." He noticed my expression change to confusion when he began the tangent. He waved off the deal on the reels and continued. "Okay, okay, doesn't matter, bro. So, I overheard them talking about going out for beers, yah know, to celebrate."

"All right…"

Cliff burped. "They're headed to Hooters."

"Hooters?"

"Hooooters," he repeated.

"That's more like it."

He raised his chin proudly. "Yup."

"Then Hooters is where we're headed."

****

We drove north across the Punta Gorda Bridge where the view overlooked the stage. Gulls were circling the tents and stages over the shrinking crowd. On the opposite side of the bridge, Charlotte Harbor was a chaos of towering waves. Sweeping wind skimmed the crests and rippled the waves crashing against the pilings of the bridge. I was glad I wasn't out there.

Cliff fumbled with the radio. "The CD player is broke."

"I'm aware," I said.

"You should get that fixed."

"One day, maybe."

"Hey, can you stop at the gas station?"

"For what?"

"Coffee," he answered.

Appreciative that Cliff was taking the first step to sobering up, I agreed to stop. Confronting Brant tonight was vital. It would be disastrous to spoon-feed them extra time, enough to make the prize money, and or a brand-new Hewes gift voucher disappear for ever.

The gas station at the base of the bridge came into sight. I figured I should top off the fuel, so I parked at a pump. Cliff rolled out and rushed for the door.

"Need anything?" he asked.

"Nope," I responded.

As I topped off the fuel, Cliff returned slurping a can of coffee espresso.

Before I could close and lock the fuel door, a glistening Mercedes rolled silently into a pump adjacent to mine. A tall, lanky, small-hunched man exited and made for the gas station doors. As he walked, his posture straightened and loosened, adjusting to the change in position. Graham Northwood.

Cliff also noticed Graham's arrival, opened the truck's passenger door, and sat. "Think he noticed us?"

"No, he went straight inside the store … didn't even look our way."

Cliff drank the coffee. "Where's he goin'?"

"I'm not sure," I said. "But we're going to find out."

"What about Brant?" Cliff asked.

"This might be the source where it all began."

"Gotcha, like the center of the universe, brother." After one last gulp and slurp, the coffee was gone. He crushed the can and tossed it out of the window into the trash bin.

We sat and waited for Graham to exit the store. I glanced at the Mercedes. Another person was sitting not quite high enough to peek over the dash.

I whispered, facing the Mercedes: "You see her?" Silence drew suspicion. I peeked at Cliff, who was dosing off. "Cliff!"

He jolted awake. "Yeah?" His eyes opened wide.

"How are you sleeping? You just drank a coffee."

"Just resting my eyes," he answered.

Back to a whisper, I motioned toward the car. "Look."

"Maybe his wife?" my friend said. "Cotton-top."

I gawked back to the woman in the Mercedes. "That *must* be the wife. Who else could it be?"

Cliff suddenly shifted in his seat and reached across my view. I flinched and dropped my hands to the steering wheel, accidentally setting off the horn.

The loud, high-pitched honk echoed throughout the pump bays and startled the white-haired woman. Her head spun our way. What she saw were two greasy, sweat-encrusted men sitting in a beat-down, older model truck staring her down while its driver wore a strange, creepy smirk on his face, waving in embarrassment.

Her repulsive expression needed no explanation. She turned her cotton-top away, faced forward, and then triggered the automatic windows—a suggestive notion—raising the tinted glass.

I said, "I guess she didn't think that was funny."

"She went straight for the window. Ha!"

"Yup—guess I blew our cover."

Cliff sat back forward, laying his arm out the window. "We just totally gave out the creepy vibe."

"You made me hit the horn. What did you expect?"

"Brother, that was an accident, and you're the one who told me to look over anyway. I was just as happy taking a nap."

"Yes, I did, but … whatever. What's really going to seem creepy is *us* following them."

"Oh, man," Cliff said. "She's going to call the cops if they spot us."

After another couple minutes of silence, Graham left the store, had an interesting spring in his step, and riding high, wore a pair of shorts that were a few sizes too small. His boney legs and knobby knees were wrinkled and bronzed dark. He twirled keys around his index finger before opening the door and methodically seating himself.

From inside the car, I kept watch, half-expecting his wife to rat us out. I sank into the seat, stared blankly ahead, trying to project innocence as someone definitely not spying. Cliff followed my lead.

"We should go."

The Mercedes' engine started, and it left the pump bay and hit US41, accelerating with smooth speed as it swept away.

"Let's go," I said.

I pondered that having both Brant and his father in one location made the confrontation more ideal— two scallops in one dive. I let Cliff in on a situation I had witnessed.

"Guess what I saw on the way back to the house, to check on Scupper?"

"What?"

"The release boat."

"Oh, yeah?"

"They were releasing alright..."

"I'm listening," he said.

"They were giving them out."

"Giving what out?"

"Fish..."

"To who?"

"To boats surrounding it," I said with an offended tone. "Like feeding squirrels at the park."

Cliff shook his head after a good thought. "That's strange."

We kept following the Mercedes up US41 at a safe distance, passing the iconic Fishin' Frank's bait shop. Ten minutes later, and with Hooters in clear view, we anticipated a blinker, but the Benz bypassed the Hooters' ramp.

In a blink, his turn signal flashed—just as expected, though not where I'd thought. He passed Hooters by two streets before making the turn. The road he chose was familiar with old routines. Years ago, a friend of mine had run a dive shop in one of the front offices there—a convenient stop back then, whenever my tanks ran low and the job was calling. The road led to rows of industrial park-type businesses. Mostly mechanics and cabinet shops, but also warehouses.

"Did you see that?" Cliff asked.

"Sure did," I said. "This is getting interesting. Any idea why he turned into the industrial park?"

Cliff yawned and adjusted his winter hat, pulling on the red cotton ball, which he strangely still wore. "Imagine if he's got a whole building full of unclaimed property back here…"

"I bet you're right," I replied, "…and you mentioned that Graham dealt with consignment property, right?"

"Absolutely," Cliff said.

"So, where better to open a consignment shop than back in a warehouse?"

"Exactly…"

I made the turn off US41. The sun had dipped below the horizon, so I flicked on the high beams and slowed to fifteen miles per hour. Numerous side roads and hidden buildings could easily be overlooked.

Dozens of blue roll-up doors lined the street-side of white buildings. I'd been overcautious to safeguarding our presence, which caused us to lose sight of the black Mercedes.

I turned onto a random side street. "I'm just going to start here. Drive around these buildings. See if we spot him."

"Sounds good, brother." Cliff placed his hands on the dash and leaned forward. "Maybe you should shut the lights off, you know, go stealth. There's still some light left."

My friend's plan had some logic—just not for this moment. We were already going slow enough to look guilty. Turning off the headlights would've made us look like we were trying to get caught. I declined simply, "Cops."

We reached the end of a cul-de-sac with no sign of the Mercedes. As I began getting tired, Cliff slapped my shoulder, jolting me from a sun-fried miasma. "Look! Look!" he whispered frantically.

"What, what?"

He was pointing through the driver's side window across my face. "Over there," he said. "Behind those sable palms. The car!"

I squinted in his direction. "Is that the Mercedes?"

"Oh, yeah … it's them alright. Got to be."

The car in question was no doubt the Mercedes.

I pulled off to the shoulder, killed the engine, and weaved my sight through the palm trees adjacent to the building, where the Mercedes had parked in front of a roll-up warehouse door. A standard-size door next to the roll-up door had a window, and through the window, a light beamed through the glass, ending when it hit the pavement outside, forming a lit square.

"Did you see them go in?" I asked.

"Nope, but where else could they go?"

The darkness began to affect my vision. "We might have to get a closer view."

"I'm down for whatever. You know that."

Funny thing was, I did know that, and even though I was sitting next to a dog-tired Cliff, I could tell he was in no matter what.

"Hey, wait here a minute," I said. "I'm going to sneak over, behind that tree and get a better look?"

Cliff inspected the overgrown sable palm with a cracked crown. "That tree? The little one?"

"Yeah … I mean, it's not *that* little, is it?"

"That tree isn't going to work," he said.

I shifted in the seat. "What do you mean, *isn't* going to work?"

"Isn't gonna work … too small. You'll stick out like a pink alligator."

Impressed, I played along: "Pink alligator?"

"Yeah, like a *pink alligator.*"

I opened the door and chuckled—asked him through the window, "Pink alligator, huh? What's gotten into you? Is the lack of sleep re-wiring your brain? You sit tight. I'll be back faster than you can think of another gem."

I made it uninterrupted and crouched thirty feet from the Mercedes' driver-side door. Its dome light was lit. Using the lit mirror from the visor was the shadow of Graham's wife. She had stayed behind.

I'd get no farther tonight—she'd definitely spot me if I tried, and if she had a gun, I'd be dead as a poached snook. I chose to salvage what little hope remained: that Brant had made it to Hooters. As I closed in on my Toyota, a pair of headlights beamed from around the corner. The vehicle turned into the same parking lot where the warehouse was and conspicuously parked next to the Benz.

"This can't be Brant," I mumbled.

Our change of events worked fine for me, and I slipped back to the palm tree and spied. A short man exited, waddling away from what appeared to be an early model Cadillac. In the low light, my eyes adjusted to see the extremity of his weight. He shuffled toward the light from the door's window. His features were hazy—but those eyebrows, thick and jet-black, were impossible to miss. It was the short, grouchy man from

Graham's party two days ago, and the same man from inside the winner's tent.

Eyebrows opened the door to the warehouse, and before he managed one step through the doorway, Graham emerged. He motioned to the man, pressing him back outside. Graham closed the door and turned a key. The light glossed their feet as the two men spoke outside. Eyebrow raised his arms, signaling a discrepancy. Graham reached into his pocket. Out came a fat brown envelope that he forced into Eyebrows chest, which he then slipped into his hip pocket without verifying the contents. Graham turned and entered the Mercedes.

I returned to the truck. The closer I got, the louder it was, that deep struggle between septum and epiglottis, pushing and pulling, their back-and-forth battle, vibrating tissues. I opened the door, sat, and slammed it shut.

"Were you sleeping again?"

"I'm up … I'm up." Cliff was groggy. "What's up? Find anything?"

"I'm not sure. Remember the guy from the party? The short one? Has the thick eyebrows?"

"Yeah, I've seen him a few other times. Comes to most…" Cliff yawned. "…of Mr. Northwood's parties."

"Well, he was there. Pulled up a few minutes ago and took an envelope from Graham."

"Money?"

"I have no idea but could be."

I drove clear of the lot and steered to US41, then we pulled into the Hooters' parking lot.

****

We had an essential vantage point while sitting in the parking lot facing the outdoor bar while Brant slammed a half-filled mug onto a laminated wooden table—a clear celebration of victory. Watching him and his submissive crew celebrate a forged victory was sickening. Twenty-five grand—or a brand-new flats boat—was no small thing. But from what I saw the night of the catering job, Graham had made enough money to last two lifetimes, and there was little doubt some of that wealth had trickled down to his son.

Cliff faced forward. "That beer looks good, bro."

"Yes, it does. How many people are there?"

"Well," Cliff said, "there's Brant and his sidekick … a few others maybe."

"The others seem like they'd fished the tournament too, no?"

"They do," Cliff replied.

Upon further situational inspection, one man among the table sent blood pumping to my head. The man who had the vital responsibility of returning the redfish to Charlotte Harbor, but decided to feed the vultures, clinked rounds with the alleged cheaters.

I nudged my chin toward the table. "The release captain is there, too."

Cliff sat up and peered to recognize the man. He didn't.

We sat in silence. For cathartic purposes, I breathed in multiple deep breaths. There was too much data to process. The interactions between Brant's friends and his team partner brewed inside of me a deep, uncontrollable curiosity.

Cliff yawned again. "I wonder if those other dudes at the table were in on the cheat?"

"I doubt it. Loose lips sink ships."

Cliff said, "If it *were* me, I wouldn't tell a soul."

"Yeah, that would be the smart thing to do. I mean criminally speaking, of course."

Brant was sitting on the same side as his tournament partner, still wearing a cobalt fishing shirt, but now wore his visor upside-down and backwards.

We sat pondering a way to confront them without producing a scene.

Cliff broke our concentration. "Hey, did I show you the pictures I took from the trophy ceremony at the tournament? You know, where they give away the checks and prize vouchers?"

"No, you didn't."

Cliff pulled out his phone and scrolled through the pictures. He smiled, handing me the phone.

The picture presented the winner's podium, standing the first, second, and third place finishers. The winners, Brant and his partner, held a large, big-money check for twenty-five thousand dollars. The third-place finishers were mirror images of Brant's team—same blond hair tucked underneath white visors, same mischievous grin, and loads of sponsor patches splattered across puffed chests. But what captured both my interest, and displeasure, were the second-place finishers—Pete and his son, Randy.

Chapter Ten

Cliff grinned as I viewed the photos, witnessing my expression turning from anger to disgust.

"Messed up, huh?"

"Big time," I said. "These guys stole first place away from two well-deserving people."

"How bad does that piss you off?" he asked, kindling my anger fire.

I peeled my eyes away from the phone and directed them back to Brant's table. "I think the time has come to get in there and show these cheaters what we've got."

"I agree, bro."

"I'm just wondering if those people with Brant are loyal enough that they would go down with him..."

"It's hard to tell right now, but maybe when we confront them, they'll give something away."

I said, "It's about nine o'clock, and judging by the continuous pitchers of beer, bedtime is a long time away."

Cliff stretched. "How many pitchers is that now … three, maybe four?"

"At least that many," I replied.

"They just keep on coming."

I shook my head. "I'm still perplexed over finding out who the second-place finishers are. And how are they involved?"

"Don't know."

"Was it a spur-of-the-moment decision?"

"Don't know."

"Or did he and his dad plan it over a long period of   time?

 "Don't know."

"Seems it would have taken at least a week to plan, maybe more. It wasn't the most elaborate scam I'd ever seen, but it worked—at least so far, right?"

"Don't know." Cliff smiled.

"How long do you think Brant and his dirty daddy had this thing planned out?"

"Don't know."

The two of us remained seated as Brant and his crew carried on with their carefree drinking. With each beer they downed, the odds of a coherent confrontation slipped further out of reach.

I turned to Cliff. "Did I tell you I ran into Randy? While checking on Scupper?"

"Nope."

"Yeah, he stopped me, and we had a talk. He'd drank a few beers by that point."

Interested, Cliff sat up. "Really? They couldn't have been back for more than an hour or two before us."

"I know, right? He must have started slammin' them as soon as he reached the dock. Anyway, he said his dad has liver failure."

"Oh man, that's horrible," Cliff replied. "That explains why he appeared so sick. Can't he get a transplant?"

"He mentioned his dad is currently on a list or something."

Cliff shifted in his seat—paused and faced forward. "Life's too short, brother."

"It is indeed," I replied. "This tournament was a bucket list kinda of thing. That's what Randy said. He wants to 'repay' us for helping him."

"That's dude of him. He seemed like a decent guy."

"Yeah, he was sort of on the pushy side earlier, but I'm going to give him a pass."

"How's he gonna repay us? Buy us beers?"

"I'm not sure, but I think we might be helping Pete and Randy out *again* before this is over."

My mouth began watering when Brant's busty waitress brought the table a platter of fried chicken wings. Cliff saw it too.

"You seein' what I'm seein'?" he asked.

I replied, "Yeah, those wings are mouthwatering."

"Not the wings. Check out who just got out of her car." He pointed toward the left side of the building, next to a pair of green waste dumpsters. "It's your veterinarian friend."

Dr. Clara crossed ahead, entered the establishment, scuttled to Brant's table, greeting his friends.

"How pathetic," I said.

"Oh…?" Cliff said, grinning.

Brant didn't get up, didn't say a word. He gave her nothing until her hand landed gently on his shoulder.

"See that?"

"Sure…"

"She could do a hundred times better than Brant."

"You think?"

"Maybe you're right, Cliff. Maybe it is the money that attracted her—wouldn't be the first time. One thing was for sure: she couldn't have a clue about her cheating ass boyfriend, Brant. She was too good for that. She'd leave in a heartbeat."

Cliff nodded politely and yawned.

The cheaters continued inhaling beer after beer, with no end in sight. I began to feel antsy, then an astute notion sprang to mind so I reached into the glovebox and found a pen. Next, I retrieved a scrap receipt and wrote down my cell number. After a second thought, I scratched out my number and shoved everything into my pocket.

"I think it's time to make a move—or at least get close."

"You think?" Cliff asked.

I opened the driver's door.

Cliff leaned excitedly. "What are you going to do?"

"You'll see, but I advise you to keep the engine running."

I stepped out of the truck, my confidence trailing behind me. Instead of heading straight for the entrance, I veered to the side of the building, stopping just in front of the massive front window. From this angle, the bar blocked my view of Brant's table—a small relief. I did my best to appear casual, to blend in. A minute passed. Then five. Finally, I saw an opening. My hand slipped into my pocket and closed around my phone. It was ready.

I peeked and saw Brant had slid over on his bench seat, stood, and made his way toward the bar door that led inside the restaurant. He weaved through the tables, stumbling, a cautious walk, picking his routes. He went to the restroom.

An opening to confront arrived. My first step through Hooter's front door was hit with a blast of air conditioning, and the spicy, deep-fried potent aroma of breaded wings. I avoided eye contact and crept toward the men's restroom.

Brant was standing at the urinal closest to the stalls. I pulled up my *Buff*, stepped to the open urinal next to him, pretended to start pissing, but instead reached for the cell phone, sorted to the video, and queued it for playback.

I said, "Close weigh-ins today, huh, bud?"

Brant straightened, clearly aware that men's room rule number one had just been broken. He didn't say a word—he didn't have to. His face wore the expression of a man personally offended by the breach. I had broken the unwritten law of no talking while pissing.

He rolled his eyes and effectively cut his piss off mid-stream. "Whatever, dude," he answered.

I turned and held up the video. "I think there's something you should see."

When he faced me, his vexing, spoiled child-like demeanor switched to fright. "U-u-uh—" he stuttered.

My *Buff* was weird for him, and he attempted to step past me. My arm straightened, blocking him. I pressed the phone close to his face. After smashing playback, the footage began. At first, he tried to disregard the video, but heard every word, realizing he was the star.

"Hey!" he said as his eyes locked on the tiny screen. "What are you—?"

"See anything familiar?" I asked.

He reached for my phone.

"Uh—not so fast," I said, and swung the phone away, though teasing a food-craved dog. I told him in a standoff-ish tone, "Not gonna happen. Plus, I have *many* copies." This was a lie. I never even thought about making copies, a huge misstep on my part. Sure, Cliff had his own footage, but mine was better. If Brant reached for the video again, this might get ugly—and he wasn't a small guy either. At right around six-foot-three, he was taller and heavier than me.

He exposed his pompous attitude immediately. "That ain't me," he said, a mouth overfilled with saliva. "You got nothin'."

"You know damned well this is you," I whispered. "I've been tracking you all day."

His eyes blinked in confusion. "Not sure what you're tryin' to do here." From his expression, he seemed resolute, focused on deniability above anything. He continued, "I don't know what you're' talking about. Why are you hiding *your* identity anyway, dude? You scared?"

He stretched to pull down my *Buff* but missed as I juked. My reaction was on point, and he noticed.

"Dude, are you some kind of perv?" His voice pointed toward the door and his register rose. "Hey, there's a perv in here!"

Someone could walk in at any moment, and I'd pushed my luck far enough. I told the blond-headed doofus, "You listen to me. I know you cheated, and this is proof. I know your dad's name is Graham Northwood and he lives in Punta Gorda … in PGI."

"That ain't true," he nodded like I'd answered a question wrong. "You've got no proof, dude!"

I waved the video again.

"And…?" he said.

Talking sense into him would be like teaching a crab to fetch me a beer. I had no other choice right now. I'd gone in without a solid plan once again, limp of a good idea.

"You better turn yourselves in," I said.

"You wish…" he mumbled. "I ain't giving you nothin', you perv!"

This guy was getting on my nerves—felt a threat might bring him around. "Do it, or I'll deliver this video straight to the tournament director."

He didn't react, so I drew a breath, swallowed my anger, and laced my words with an intense whisper, "And all the news companies that will listen. Think I'm joking? Try me..." This got the reaction for which I was hoping. He was finally getting a clue.

His voice dropped down to normal. "What do you want anyway?" He gently crossed his arms as if making a serious negotiation. "Money? Is that it?"

I looked him in the eye, at a loss for words. If nothing else, I was sure of this—I'd get justice for Randy and his sick father. I said, "Turn yourselves in, give the prizes to the rightful winners. Pete and Randy."

His eyes sprung open, then settled, and he grinned mischievously.

I waved the phone again. "I have the video!" Boy, was this guy stupid.

He became more confident than ever. "Whatever … doesn't prove anything."

"Oh, but it does!"

He had a fleeting thought and clenched his jaw.

I was seriously winging it, and was somehow winning, but time became a factor as someone could walk in any moment and disrupt us, so our private meeting appeared to be almost over. I pushed. "I'm waiting…"

"You got nothin'."

This guy was tiring me out. I reached down my pocket and whipped out the paper and pencil. "Give me your phone number." I readied the pen and paper, anticipating his response.

It was an easy out for him. He had to take it.

I took his number and told him flat-out—come up with a solution, and fast, or he'd regret it.

He shrugged off the threat as the spoiled kid he was. "Whatever, dude," were his exact words.

In a flash, I bolted from the men's room and fled toward the exit, incognito, but saw a very familiar face. Dr. Clara was weaving through tables, heading straight for me. Before I could dodge her, our eyes met.

I met Dr. Clara on a charter, which she gave her dad for his fiftieth birthday. We were a perfect match—at least I thought. She was tall, brunette, and had one the most gorgeous sets of shoulder blades I'd ever seen. We did everything together: went to Devil Rays games, she went with me on pre-charter scouts, I even taught her the basics of throwing a cast net on the grass flats outside Burnt Store Marina. Extremely intelligent woman—went to Brown University, then on to vet school at USF. After graduation, she returned home to Sanibel Island to visit family and decide the trajectory of her next phase in life.

That same day she'd caught a monster dark-skinned gag grouper on a new man-made reef I'd stumbled upon months prior. And hours after the charter she'd called and asked if I'd heard of any new recipes for the fish she'd caught. After a brief ponder, I realized it was an invite. Not usually an entertainer, I was still compelled to invite Dr. Clara and her father for dinner, you know, just friendly gesturing that any polite fishing guide would do. In garlic butter, we glazed the grouper and bathed it in egg wash, finishing in homemade breadcrumbs. We let the olive oil fry it until golden brown, and finally, resting it on a bed of brown rice, I served her fish with white wine.

After the first fillets were cooked, Dr. Clara commandeered the cooking while her dad and I enjoyed a beer.

She'd been wearing her hair in a ponytail, skin free of makeup. A clear, tan neck exposed underneath a sunflower-printed summer dress. I studied her meticulous handling of the fish using only fingertips.

She tolerated me and my laid-back mentality, and she didn't seem to mind that the yard was a wreck, my clothes were balled up on the floor, and the kitchen floor was a little sticky, she understood me. We dated off and on for a few months, but it always fizzled out.

"Shamus?"

I was busted. She somehow recognized me.

"Hey," I said, shaking out the daydream.

She said with a bashful grin, "I recognize those eyes…"

I pulled the *Buff* down halfway, made a step toward the door. "I bet, but listen, I'm in a hurry."

"Oh, okay," she said, pulling back. "I'm just having a few beers … with friends."

She didn't say with Brant. She was concealing it from me.

"I see…" I checked the bathroom doors.

"So, yeah, how's Samantha? I mean Scupper, sorry."

I really had no time for a conversation. "Never been better. Listen, I've got to run. Talk to yah later."

"Oh, okay."

As she brushed passed, I caught a soft whiff of perfume, the same kind she wore when we dated. I felt a gleaming flicker of pride knowing that we had history. I felt like no matter what, I knew things about her that Brant could only dream. The thought hit me hard, flooding back memories of the two of us making love on cold examining tables. I turned enough to see if she had glanced back, but all I saw was the closing of the women's room door.

Back outside, I opened my truck's door, and to my surprise, Cliff was wide-awake playing a game on his phone.

He stayed silent and waited for me to begin a conversation. I started the truck and drove from the parking spot when a dark silhouette stumbled ahead of the truck. I hit the brakes. Headlights blinding, the man continued on with just a "my fault wave."

Cliff slapped my shoulder. "Look!"

"What?" I asked.

"It's Randy!"

Cliff was correct. Randy crossed our path in a drunken stupor.

I mumbled, "That kid gets around, doesn't he?"

"You ain't lying," Cliff responded.

He staggered off toward the front doors and was gone. We hit US41 and drove south toward Punta Gorda.

Cliff said, "So, how did it go?"

"Let's just say he got caught with his pants down."

Chapter Eleven

The following morning, Sunday, an ear-piercing yelping flung me up from my air mattress bed. Stubbing my toe on the door jamb, I stumbled for the kitchen half-asleep, brain focused on one thing—finding the source and eliminating it. I made my way through the kitchen and into the dining room, where Scupper's face was pressing against the glass, leaving wet blotches of an outlined nose. I made a visual sweep of the backyard to find the basis of her attraction.

"What is it, girl?"

Scupper continued whining while I opened the sliding door, and then the lanai screen door. She bolted off, heading straight for the dock. As I observed, I felt she was in good hands, or fins.

After the coffee brewed, I meandered the yard to see what the big deal was. The sun was rising on a slow track to the north as I breathed in waves of sultry air.

After a short walk, I saw no sign of the pooch. From atop the houseboat roof deck, I panned across the basin's oily slick glass top. In the distance, mullet breached from the underworld, and further off, charter guides motored past the mouth, heading for client pick-up.

I heard Scupper's distinctive bark reverberating across the basin. She was standing paw-deep on the small shoal at the head of the basin. Spinner was circling her in a rigid arch, thrusting up its tail. "Unbelievable."

Scupper's ears perked when she heard my voice, and she sniffed the air while I waved and called her name. "Over here you crazy dog."

During the easy idle toward the bar to retrieve her, I puttered upon Flip's house. One single porch light was lit, and his twenty-four-foot Sheffield no longer appeared abandoned—someone had been cleaning it up. I continued toward Scupper.

Long ago, this basin became filled with a patchwork of oyster beds and deceptive sandbars. At low tide, you'd be a fool to enter without reading the water. As I approached Scupper and called, her tail wagged as she carelessly leaped into the water. I cringed at the damage sharp oysters might inflict. While she swam my way, Spinner submerged.

I lifted Scupper's wet body into the skiff by the collar, then puttered toward my dock. After we bumped the houseboat's pontoon, she hopped off, trotted overtop the houseboat's front deck, and onto the rickety plank. She then did what dogs do and shook herself dry.

"Come on, girl," I said, and walked the plank onto solid ground, and in doing so glanced at Flip's house.

"He must be back," I mumbled. Flip's house could only be seen from the first few feet after stepping off the plank. After that, it was mostly overgrown grass, untrimmed sable palms, and minor palmetto thickets.

Back at the house, I sipped coffee and fed Scupper.

The plan for the day was simple: do some needed maintenance on my charter rods and ponder the next move with Brant.

After both RV-sized garage doors were raised, I set up a folding table. First step: separating the reels from the rods—four of them. After spreading them on a cotton towel, I began removing the spools. Next, I dislodged the bail-nut lock. I tend to buy the best I can, but when clients get their hands on them, anything can happen. The next step was locating a grease brush and oil pen that I knew I kept in a red Craftsman's toolbox under a bunch of clutter.

I'd only just begun to indulge in the stillness when a diesel engine thundered nearby, shaking my focus from the rod. Flip Peas had pulled up the driveway and parked behind my truck. I raised, found the grease and oil, and sat back on the plastic chair. After he shut down the Dodge's engine, it sputtered for a few seconds, ticked for a few more, then settled still and quiet.

Flip's hands were fisted inside his oversized white overalls. He appeared more like a farmer than a mullet fisherman. "Saw you floatin' awn by ... pickin' up that pooch," he said, stepping into the garage. "She sure had taken a likin' to that pesky dolphin hangin' 'round the canal."

"You saw that?"

"Sure did." His eyes slanted. "I'm not a fan of dolphins competin' for my mullet." He then smiled.

Flip left his hands in the pockets. His shirt was a thin, sea-green tee tucked down denim overalls. Same white beard, same raspy voice. "I recognize that pooch alright," he said slowly. "Seen her trottin' down Burnt Store Road few months back. "About ran'er over."

"That would be her…" I lowered the tools, leaned back. "So, when did you get back in town?"

"Oh … late last night."

I nodded sincerely. After a few awkward seconds, I realized the elephant in the room wasn't going anywhere. "So, how have you been?"

"Good, good," he said, scanning over my pile of parts. He needn't explain anything, we both knew what I meant. Eliot, who was killed last year, for many years, had been Flip's good buddy. Around here, that meant something extremely profound.

I could tell his answer was a lie, so I didn't push. "I see … I see. I wasn't sure if you were coming back *or* not."

"I almost wasn't goin' to, but what I've come ta'undastand is what happened awn that day was completely out of m'control." He looked at me, and added, "And yours. Someone, or *somethin'*—God, the devil, or *whatever*, stepped in awn that day and changed m'life forever."

I replied, "I've gone through it a million times, and I see a million things I should have done different—"

"No!" He eased closer to the table. "Shamus, I knew Eliot longer than you been 'live. We went to high school together. Him and I, started off fishin' awn the same mullet boat long ago. Back then, you kept a few friends—about all one could handle."

"I under—"

He raised his hand. "Now let me go ahead and finish." His tone was now ominous. "I don't blame yah for what happened, and from this day forward, I don't want you to blamin' yourself either. Out there, yah did what yah could. There was no other outcome, you hear?"

I owed him a straightforward response. "I do." I wouldn't argue with Flip on this, but there were things I could've done differently that might have resulted in Eliot still being alive. Flip's conviction was strong, and I realized he'd thought about it for a long time. His decision wasn't mine to undermine. "Well, I'm glad you're back."

"Who was I kiddin', I couldn't leave 'is town even if I tried," he said with a smirk, went on, "Mullet fishin' … it's in m'blood. The wife and I went up to Ohio. Stayed with her family, and let me tell yah, not somethin' I'd wish awn m'worst enemy."

"Must have had nice weather?"

He answered as if trying to switch subjects: "Yeah, yeah. It wasn't bad … nothin' like Flor'da, though."

"I bet."

He eyed my spread of reels and different parts. "Cleanin' up some gear, are we?"

"Sure am. These Penns…" I reached for one. "Take a massive beating. I'm not sure if I should start putting floats on them or what."

Flip showed a "been there, done that" smirk. "Uh-huh."

"I've had a few hit the drink recently … if you know what I mean."

His expression told me he did. "You keep awn cleaning them. They'll take gooood care of yah for a long, long time. Penn … they good reels."

Flip watched me clean the spindle gear delicately using a small brush. I battled the decision to get his advice on the current Graham and Brant situation. I told myself I wouldn't involve him in anything dangerous ever again. But did this qualify as dangerous? I did, however, need his opinion on a newly discovered event.

"Can I ask you a question?"

His chin raised in interest. "Shoot."

"How do you feel about by-catch?"

"By-catch?" he questioned. "Like accidental catches?"

I nodded.

"Well, yah need a special license to keep 'em…" He wanted more information. I gave him the scoop on what I had witnessed.

He smiled. "Always got your ear to the ground, on the pulse of the earth, don't yah?"

I nodded genuinely.

"But those Fish?" Flip said. "Them dead."

Not the answer I was expecting. "Dead?" I asked skeptically. "Really?"

"Yup, those release guys been givin' those away f'years.

I didn't look convinced.

He raised his bearded chin, so I'd pay closer attention. "See, Shamus, he's prolly tossin' the ones that he finds floatin' belly up in the tank out to those guys first."

I thought for a second. The transactions on the release boat were swift and impossible to tell if the redfish were dead or alive.

He said semi-sternly, "Let 'em have the dead ones. At least they'll get eaten."

"This is true, but those fish wouldn't have died if those teams hadn't caught them."

His mouth pressed shut, and he moistened his lips. "That's a goooood point, Shamus."

"So, you see the problem?"

"I do, to'lly. They just by-catch. Somethin'll eat 'em. Back before the net ban, we had plenty of by-catch. It'd get caught up in the over-sized mesh holes and, yes, some'd die. They just became food in the grass f'the crabs and pinfish."

I was still frustrated. Flip knew it.

"Listen, son, people gawn do what they gawn do. You can't change'at. Some of the hardcore commercial guys, they haven't the ability to reason ... morally, speakin'. Everthin' *allriiight* in their heads. Maybe it's gene'ic, prolly parentin'. Who knows, really…"

"I know, but these tournaments—"

"Hell, to this day, commercial guys get caught all time draggin' nets … some doin' a clean sweep of an entire bar. Hurts the honest guy, too. But like I say, gawn do what they gawn do."

I shook my head.

He went on, "Conservation's a fickle bitch. The smart guy knows what conservation means and how it can b'done correctly. They undastand that if yah take too much, they'll b'nothin' left. Others too, might know this, but like I say, gawn do what they gawn do."

"You'd think they'd want to preserve … it's their livelihood, too…"

"They're prolly too broke to care."

****

The reels were over-cleaned.

Flip then stroked his white seaman's beard and molded it to a point. "Noticed the ol' houseboat out back there. New toy?"

I stepped through the roll-up garage door and lined the houseboat in sight. "Yup, it's not one-hundred-percent mine. It's a partnership with a good buddy from North Carolina. He purchased it and asked if I'd moor it in the canal. He insisted that I use it from time to time."

"You go awn ahead and let me know if yah take 'er out anytime soon." He winked.

"Will do. Will do."

"Okay, got to head awn out," he said, and stuck out his hand.

"It was good seeing you." We shook hands.

"It's good to be back awn in town, I'll tell yah." He slid a few steps toward his truck. "I gotta head off into town, to the post office, pick up the mail." He measured his hand shoulder high." Prolly a big ol' pile of it waitin' I'm sure."

"But it's Sunday, Flip … pretty sure they're closed."

His janitorial-size key ring swung up by a finger. "P.O. box. All yah need is the key."

His feet hit the gravel rimming the garage's foundation and he moseyed to his truck. He pulled away, honked once, signaling making way.

I greased, oiled, and attached the reels back on the rods, and then aligned them by size onto my rotating custom rod holder. I went back into the house to pour another cup of coffee.

When I entered the house, Scupper began barking fanatically, forcing her nose against the sliding glass door.

"You want to go out?"

Her head lifted at me, wagging her tail as a pink, meaty tongue pulsed and dangled from the corner of her mouth.

I spoke to the pooch as though she understood the reasoning. "What am I going to do with you? You can't go out and swim with Spinner all day. You'll drown." After I finished the last sentence, Sara's words flashed on a mental projection screen, "*She could possibly drown!*" I remembered her telling me. Never thought she'd get inside my head, but it appeared she'd snuck past a highly guarded conscience. Speaking of Sara, I opened my phone and sent her a text:

Meet for lunch?

After ten minutes a reply came back: *Okay! Where?*

Gribbles 12 p.m?

Fine!

The exclamation point after a normal response was an obvious attempt at flattery.

I opened the door to the lanai, allowing Scupper only as far as the screen door of the quaint lanai. Her nose lifted to sniff out the swimming mammal.

"What an unlikely companionship," I said.

I predicted that this uncanny friendship between her and the dolphin might cause me more than a few future headaches, so I had to think of a method to make the situation safer. Could I fence off the ramp? Maybe fencing off the dock was a possibility? I doubted she would jump in the water from the seawall, but if she did, and the ramp was fenced, she'd most likely become shark bait. But would the dolphin allow it? I finished off a cup of coffee.

Before meeting Sara at Gribbles for lunch, I carved out a minute to check my charter schedule I kept in a spiral notebook. I tried to schedule charters on Mondays, Tuesdays, and Wednesdays, to leave the rest of the week off for downtime and soul-searching. Tomorrow being Monday, I had an uncommon morning charter at six a.m—couldn't pass up the money.

I began a brief brainstorm for my upcoming trip on the way to the dock. If by chance the tide wasn't moving much tomorrow, which slows down the bite, I'd certainly reschedule or explain the situation to the client. After I saw the "six o'clock," I checked the tides and realized that the outgoing tide indeed started from a +1.2 at 6:04 a.m. Just enough time to get out, catch bait, and be ready in time for the clients.

I dawdled to the dock and noted the height in the fuel cell. Scupper began barking from inside the house.

Soft-hearted me retreated to the door and let her out. I yelled, "HEY," after she darted off to the dock. She slowed, stopped, and returned to my side, tail between her legs.

"It's okay," I told her, and scratched her head. "You can't go running down there like that." I just realized I had become one of those crazies who talk to their pet and think they understand it. Dogs were more sensitive to tone, not specific words—and I knew that.

Scupper trotted close by my side; nose held up in the air. Her long pink tongue lolled off to the side of her lower jaw, dangling as she drew heavy breaths. She hit the front deck of my skiff and sniffed the water, sort of a smell radar, back and forth, directing her wet, convex nostrils.

"I'm not sure she's around, girl."

The fuel cell was three-quarters full, and with the sixty-horsepower engine I ran, fuel economy was unbelievable. With a filled medium-sized seventeen-gallon fuel tank, I'd run unstressed across the harbor all day. I stepped off the skiff to the houseboat and onto the dock.

Back in the house, I showered and washed for lunch with Sara. Had I figured what to do about Scupper's dolphin obsession, I'd be more inclined to leave her out, but for now she remained on house arrest.

I drove off my street at moderate speed, hit Burnt Store Road, and headed toward Downtown Punta Gorda. My window was down, my arm hung out, and after hearing Jimmy Hendrix, I cranked the radio up. I thought about Graham, and the warehouse meeting, and the man sporting those thick eyebrows, and how it would be beneficial to get a healthy peek inside the secret warehouse. The peculiar meeting there last night was concerning. The two men had gathered at what seemed to be a legitimate place of business, then spoke to each other the way two men meeting in secret would, then one handed the other a fat, suspicious envelope. Possessing the information that I had, my dubious reaction felt justified. Shamus Pickford was no rat, but on occasion, was a quizzical S.O.B.

It would be wise for anyone driving Burnt Store Road to apply extra caution and pin a steady eye ahead. Its narrowness and lack of a median didn't couple with the spotty streetlights. Off to the sides of the road, overgrown Brazilian Pepper trees filled the shoulders, extending lanky, green-leafed branches on the verge of impeding the roadway. Many a critter had been sent to another dimension trying to cross Burt Store Road. Multiple mailboxes also protruded out into the street, mostly standard black, store-bought boxes that sat atop wooden posts. Others were more decorative—a bloated manatee and oversized flamingo beaks that housed large mail. There was even a largemouth bass big enough to swallow a small child.

Nearly ten minutes later, I tailed behind a dark-tinted red Chevy Colorado. Its speed fluctuated from ten mph below to five mph above the posted speed limit, which was fifty-five miles per hour. For seconds at a time, it slowed, then sped. The license plate was a tarpon-imaged Florida Fish and Wildlife Conservation Commission vanity plate and read WSH1FSHN.

It continued swerving for five minutes until the vehicle's brake lights flashed and it crossed the center line, slewing toward the shoulder. I stomped on the brake pedal and the reason for the slew became clear. Plumes of brown and white feathers spewed from under the truck and fluttered to the asphalt. Out of a mid-air flight, the red Colorado had hit a large, low crossing bird.

Stunned, I sat. This desolate stretch of road was built back in a time that didn't warrant sidewalks. What I witnessed next was more shocking than the act itself. The Colorado continued, swerving brashly into its original lane.

I had but a nanosecond to decide whether to chase the truck or to check the blatantly injured animal. Ahead, the truck had gained a mile, only a red smudge was visible through the heat waves rising off the street. I decided to check the scene to find the animal.

Cars began to arrive, slowing and rubbernecking as I approached the suspected area. I searched thoroughly where the blurred ball of feathers fell from the sky. Laying in the swale twenty feet from the road, an injured great horned owl blinked a set of big eyes back at me. The bird's eyes were huge, and its tiny yellow irises stared back at me while it backstroked frantically, trying to flee. Sadly, as it flapped its wings, one dangled limp and loose, meaning this owl wasn't going anywhere.

I left the scene, and at my truck, in a toolbox, I found a pair of old batting gloves for protection that had been doubling as mechanic's gloves. I put them on and brought an old towel from the back seat.

Shocker, the bird was uncooperative. Every step closer I slipped, the raptor flapped its wings manically, sweeping backward, sending clouds of loose feathers into the air. Its damaged wing now exposed white bone. I rushed in, snatched it by its good wing and clamped both wings shut, pressing it close to my chest.

After securing its razor-sharp talons, I held it by the legs away from my body. The owl bent its neck to hold its head stiff to keep right-side-up.

As I carried it to the truck, I heard faint voices. "Oh look, an owl … he's got an owl!" I ignored the chatter, opened the truck's door, and gently tossed the bird inside. It landed on the passenger floorboard, staring at me—wide as could be—little yellow iris, black as death—penetrating down to the soul. It wanted to peck my eyes out.

"Don't you know I'm here to help you?"

It answered in a shrieking squeal that would have surprised even the most knowledgeable ornithologist. Back on the road, I drove to the Peace River Wildlife Center, a non-profit organization, located at Ponce de Leon Park. For obvious reasons, I decided not to take it to Dr Clara's clinic.

****

The drive to the Wildlife Center had its challenges when the owl decided that multiple attempts to escape through the passenger side window would benefit its survival.

At the center, the wonderful volunteers determined the owl had a broken wing and required a visit to the vet. They offered to oversee it from there and gave me a free T-shirt.

I left the center, made a U-turn, and passed the boat ramp. Before pulling out onto W. Marion Ave, I felt the subtle vibration of an incoming text message.

I had missed four messages—all from Sara.

I'm here...

Hello?!?

Are you coming?

I've got to get back to work!

The last one made me think she would not be waiting for me at Gribbles. I hit the gas and sped the whole way to the deli. I arrived fifteen minutes later and my entrance about knocked the bells off the door.

The deli was roughly the size of a small Chinese takeout joint—strip mall-style. A counter for ordering began ahead, the menu above. Four tables lay against the front window that could seat two people apiece. I had bought a fake, life-sized mount of a six-foot tarpon a few years ago and thought it would present well on the side wall above the drink cooler—it did.

Cliff stood at the counter assisting a customer. I brushed by the front counter, slipped behind the sandwich prep table, and kept walking until I reached a small office that was no bigger than a corporate cubicle, just big enough for a computer and the pile of paperwork stacked beside it. It had no A/C. I found my phone and stood next to Cliff.

"She's gone," he said.

"Yeah, figured." I walked past him toward the counter. "Something came up."

Cliff reached for a log of salami, laid it on the sandwich counter atop a cutting board and began to slice multiple thin, bread-sized circles.

I dialed Sara's number, then whispered to Cliff, "She's going to be *pissed*." It rang three times, and went to voicemail, just the right amount of time for her to retrieve the phone, view the caller ID, and hit the ignore button. I didn't leave a voicemail message and hung up.

I then sent a quick text:

Rescued an owl

Sorry I missed our lunch date

More details later

On the way out, I asked Cliff, "On a scale of one to ten, how pissed was Sara when she left?"

Cliff had now sliced three-quarters through the salami log. "Not too pissed."

"Like a five or a six?" I asked.

"Yeah, I'd say that's about right, brother. I made her a soft, grass-fed beef burger topped with spinach and pepper jack cheese for lunch."

"Really? Damn, you should whip me up one of those."

Cliff reached in the cooler and returned cupping a baseball-size chunk of well-seasoned beef. It sizzled after he slapped it on the flattop grill.

"Did she like it?"

"Pretty sure," Cliff said. "She ate half, took the rest."

My back faced the beef ball on the grill while I told Cliff the situation about the owl, and the reason I was late for lunch with Sara.

"She'll get over it once I explain it to her," I said, weak in confidence.

"Yeah—no worries. I wouldn't stress over it. Like I said, she was a five or a six."

"I should have known," I said. "I knew she had to work, so the window for lunch was tiny."

Cliff finished off the salami log after a hard chop of the knife. The burger's scent rose. My stomach noticed and began growling.

"That smells great."

"You want cheese?" he asked.

"Pepper jack, please."

Cliff laid the fresh cheese slice on the flattened beef ball, and it began to melt.

After minutes of sizzling, I removed the burger, laid it on a toasted bun, took a substantial bite, and explained the owl scenario.

"So, the person just ran off and didn't stop?" Cliff asked.

"You are correct," I replied.

"Why didn't you chase him? Sounds like a Shamus scenario."

After a liberal bite of the burger, I gave a full-mouth answer: "I wish, but I had to attend to the dying bird on the side of the road. Believe me, I'd love to have followed them and given them a piece of my mind. There's no fault in hitting an animal by accident—could have happened to anyone. But taking off and not checking on it? Just wrong, man. No matter how you calculate it, just wrong."

Cliff held a bottle of spray cleaner and was now wiping down the front of the stainless-steel fryer. "I agree. Karma, brother … it'll catch up to him."

"One can only hope."

Cliff slipped to a side counter and continued wiping. "Any word on Brant and *that* situation?"

"No, I haven't made the call. I want to give them time—but not too much time. Truth is, I have no idea what to do."

"Right, right," Cliff said, then eyed me. "I bet he's gettin' rid of the money as we speak."

I ate the last of the burger and lowered the plate into the dishwasher rack. "He better not be. As far as I'm concerned, that money doesn't belong to him."

"Who *does* it belong to then?" Cliff challenged.

"Good question. I'm not sure."

"Randy and Pete?" he asked.

"It's possible…"

"You could wait until tomorrow to call them."

"Can't. Tomorrow I've got an early charter. These guys want to catch big snook, and you know what that means…"

"More work for you?"

"Well, kinda. I'm waking at five a.m., running across the harbor to Cape Haze Point for bait. The other day I saw small schools of threadfins. Those in the baitwell will do perfectly. After bait, I'll double back, pick them up at the boat ramp at Ponce, no later than eight a.m."

"Big-wigs?" he asked, hand rotating against the stainless-steel.

"Yeah, hot-shot Executives. They pre-paid. Sent a check … big money."

"So, business is picking up?"

"It's steady, that's for sure. I'm not turning people away by any means, but as of right now I'm able to book three days a week."

Now that lunch had been canceled, I decided to spend the rest of the day at the deli and help Cliff.

After three hours of preparing meals and helping customers, I had heard no word from Sara.

Cliff walked up as I finished assisting the last customer, cracked a beer, and handed one to me.

I drank. "It seems like business is picking up here, too."

"Steady. Can't complain."

For a moment my mind switched focus, and I thought about Scupper and if, at this exact moment, her nose was pressed up against the lanai door. Maybe I could lure the dolphin away somehow? The last thing I wanted for Scupper was to be tied up in the house, or out in the yard. She needed to be able to roam and be free.

I finished the beer and tossed it in the trash, hitting another bottle. Cliff asked if I'd like to make a sandwich for tomorrow. I said yes and whipped up a simple turkey on wheat.

I asked. "What time are you closing tonight?"

"Around seven p.m."

When I heard Cliff say seven p.m., I decided *that's* when I'd make the call.

Cliff and I scrubbed all the equipment and tightly wrapped the deli meats. After I brought in the sidewalk sign, I found the small receipt paper I'd scribbled Brant's number on, went to the office, and dialed it after pressing star six seven. It rang three times, then a voice on the other end: "Hello?"

"So—" I coughed out of reluctance and had to gather my voice and begin again. "So … have you thought about what we discussed?"

"Who is this?" the voice asked suspiciously.

"You know who *this* is…"

He paused. "What do you want, dude?"

"I think you know what I want."

"You won't give up, will you?"

"I will not. You cheated. You don't deserve the prize."

"You can't prove—"

"I have you on video, *dude!*" I was being firm with him, and it seemed to be working.

Another long pause from him proved my message received.

Before he replied, I added, "I'm not playing. Have you figured out what I'm getting at?" Asking this, I wasn't confident Brant had the brain power to solve his current predicament. What did I really expect him to say? That he'd return the money no problem?

"I need more time," Brant finally said.

"You're out of time.

"Call me back in one hour," he said with a heavy breath into the phone. "Okay, dude?"

"You better not play games with me."

"No games … just call me back in one hour."

I paused but agreed. "You've got one hour." I ended the call.

Chapter Twelve

I arched back in the chair, hands behind my head, reflecting on the conversation. I didn't have a clue as to what I expected Brant to say. I enjoyed toying with him. What was the harm in letting him squirm for a little while? Or was he making me squirm? I headed out to the front counter, where Cliff held the day's purse.

"Good day?" I asked.

"Not bad, not bad," he replied, counting the cash like a bank teller.

I told him, "So I called Brant."

Sill counting the cash, he peeked up. "Oh, yeah?"

"Yup."

Cliff finished counting the cash and placed it into a bank bag and zipped it. "So, what's the deal with Brant then?"

"He wants me to call him back in one hour."

"That's what he said?"

"Yup."

He led to the rear exit door to lock up. "You going to call him?"

"Absolutely I'm going to call him. As much as I'd like it to be, this thing *ain't* over."

Cliff asked the obvious question: "How are you going to solve this without gettin' identified? You might need to meet him, brother—in person, eventually."

"Good point. I'm not ruling out meeting him in person again. I'll just wear the *Buff* again—" This time I couldn't hold back laughter.

"You can't wear that to a meeting. You'd look like a maniac."

Cliff was right. If I didn't make the right moves, I'd have to meet Brant again, in person. At the front of the deli, Cliff killed the lights and double-checked the meat cooler doors. Then we left.

We passed multiple flats boats attached to reflective new pickups while walking to the parking garage. The tournament teams and their guests usually spend the weekend in town.

As we walked a short sidewalk toward the two-story parking garage, a dozen trucks towing boats drove by, dripping water from their drain holes.

We reached the ramp to the parking garage's second-floor deck. I told Cliff to keep his ears on, and that I would contact him after the arrival of any new developments. He agreed and we parted ways.

****

It had been far too long since the last word from Sara, so I checked my messages, finding none.

The walk up the ramp inside the parking garage had just the amount of exertion necessary to send small sweat beads trickling down my temple. Even in the evening hours, Florida's humidity was out to kill.

I arrived at the truck, retrieving my cell phone and the receipt where I'd written Brant's number. I began dialing, then stopped, wondering if calling from the personal cell was a smart move. Even privatizing the number using star six seven like before, if Brant wanted it bad enough, methods existed to recover it.

I decided to use a payphone, but an obstacle was in the way—I wasn't sure where to find one. In present-day America, every man, woman, and child owned a cell phone, so payphones had gone obsolete, practically vanishing. I ran through various locations in my head where I might have seen payphones. A distorted picture popped into my mind—a vague image of one at Gilchrist Park in Punta Gorda, just a short five-minute drive away. It was a chance worth taking.

Dusk approached as I arrived at the park. Unperturbed couples walked hand in hand along the harbor ahead of the dimming light. Gilchrest Park was eleven acres along Charlotte Harbor amid the Peace River, your casual emblematic waterfront Florida Park—tennis courts, playgrounds, swings, and of course equipping a well-used fishing pier.

I parked the truck, soaked in the panoramic view, and breezed toward the seawall leading to the fishing pier where multiple groups of fishermen spread out. The first few men down the pier were using cast nets to collect bait, mullet, or crab in the shallows. The next group consisted of people leaning on their elbows, tipping over the railing, guarding baited lines. Others toward the end of the pier were mixed between fishermen and cast netters, and they too leaned over the wooden railing while lowering lanterns and well-lit lights.

Up ahead, I spotted the phone booth next to the tennis courts. Inside, the receiver was cracked, and the earpiece had been smashed and smelled like vomit.

"This thing better work," I mumbled.

I pressed the pickup switch, and a dial tone buzzed in the earpiece. After sliding a quarter into the slot, I dialed Brant's number. No answer. "Dammit."

I slammed the receiver down, and the quarter clinked back through the return slot. I stood in the booth for a few seconds, then decided to try again. Still no answer. Frustrated, I stepped out and started toward the pier— then the phone rang behind me.

Brant must have screened the call. Caller ID was standard on most cell phones, so no surprise there.

I answered the phone and said, "What's your plan?"

No immediate answer. On the other end of the line, heavy rustling and muting streamed through the cracked microphone, then a muffled voice emitted while two people were discussing something. A man cleared his throat.

"Hello? Hello? Who is this?"

Confusion set me on a pause. This voice wasn't the same spoiled brat character as before. The voice wasn't Brant's. The man on the other end was Graham Northwood.

"Where is Brant?" I asked the man.

He cleared his throat again. "I'll ask the questions, thank you."

It appeared Brant had done what any weak person would do—called daddy to fight his battle. It wasn't too surprising though, being that Graham might be the mastermind behind the whole plan. Weak-minded people are like electrical current: they follow the path of least resistance.

"Mr. Northwood, I assume?"

"Now—how did you know my name? Do I know you?"

I disguised my voice with a low, futile whisper. "Trust me, you don't know me."

"Uh-huh … your voice sounds familiar. But regardless, what do you want, sir?"

I paused. I had met the man, once, in person. At his old age, could he recognize my voice over the phone? There was no reason for me to suspect after meeting him, however brief it had been, that he had any hindering memory issues.

I disregarded the statement. "I'm sure your son has informed you of the current situation, no?"

"Why yes, he has."

"Well?" I asked.

"Listen, let's be adults about this. I propose we resolve this in person … have an adult conversation and discuss our solution over a drink. What do you say, sir?"

Graham's tone indicated a week sense of seriousness, and his request confirmed my suspicion that he was, if not the mastermind, at least implicated in the scam. Also, that Brant had conveyed the situation correctly.

Before I could answer, a background voice through the phone sounded like Brant. He mentioned the warehouse. I pressed the vomit-scented cracked earpiece against my head, focused all the attention through a small group of holes. Again, muffled talk, and then, "Hello? Are you still there?"

"Yes, I'm here," I answered.

"So, what about that drink?"

Mr. Northwood was attempting to prove something here, but I wasn't sure what it was. His voice had softened to a light and gentle tone, but his offer to meet could be a trap.

Knowing that he had cheated Pete and Randy out of first place, it was hard to believe that Graham—or Brant, or both—hadn't applied the same unethical tactics to other areas of their lives. More important areas, such as business deals that required the same level of Machiavellianism.

"Okay," I said. "A meeting will be fine."

"Good," he said, as though he wasn't used to waiting. "You just bring what you showed my son, and we'll figure something out." It felt similar to a verbal scrimmage, and I knew that he'd request the video.

"Where?" I asked.

"Are you familiar with Port Charlotte?"

'Sure am."

"Across from Hooters there is an industrial park. I have a warehouse. We can discuss our situation there. Sound okay?" Graham had a way in his delivery that projected authority. I drew caution, realizing this wasn't his first rodeo, yet I was lured into it by some arcane attraction, regardless of its potential danger.

"Yes, I'm aware of the place."

"Then ten p.m. it is."

"Fine," I answered, and then hung up.

I left the booth and hurried back to the truck. I dialed Cliff's number and waited. No answer after ten rings.

Graham's meeting was still a couple hours away, so I headed back to the house to check on Scupper. On the way, I stopped at the local department store to pick up a brainstormed gift, something to ease Sara's contempt when Scupper wished to swim.

****

Back home, I fed Scupper and out she went to do her thing. A dusky stroll along the path leading to the dock led to a check of the mooring lines on the skiff. I undid and started the dock rope to a figure-eight, followed by a half-hitch, securing the skiff to the cleat on the bow of the houseboat.

Before heading up to the house, I noticed Scupper sniffing the air. "I don't see your buddy anywhere." Her tail wagged, and I swore she understood what I said.

Across the open basin, I beamed the flashlight, projecting a broad ray of controlled light. "Nope, no dolphin," I said to the dog.

I checked my phone again—no messages, then wisely decided to call Sara.

After five rings, she answered. "Hello?"

I wasted no time. "Are you upset?"

A deep breath on the other end, followed by, "Nooooo, why would I be?"

This question, a clear trap, had only one acceptable answer. "Because I missed lunch, that's why."

"No, Shamus, I'm not mad, just…"

"Just what?" I asked.

"Just disappointed. Thought we could have a nice lunch."

"I know, but don't you want to know why I missed it?"

"I know why. I got your text."

"Listen, it happened so quick. This truck in front of me hit an owl and just left it for dead on the side of the road. I had no choice."

"Shamus, I'm not upset that you had to save an animal. I'm upset because you didn't give me a head's up and just left me waiting at Gribbles like an idiot."

"You're right … it was inconsiderate of me not to call. For that I apologize."

"Thank you. I appreciate that."

"Again, my apologies."

Her tone went soft and had a vulnerable quality. "You could make it up to me…"

"Oh, really?"

"Are you at the house?"

"I am, but I'm on my way out for a little while. Umm…" I really was an idiot.

After a resounding sigh, she said, "Don't worry about it … it's no big deal."

Sara's attitude penetrated straight to the heart as her mounting disappointment seeped through the phone. I asked myself: Was there a reason I kept the circumstances with Graham from her? If I questioned her one more time about it, it might start an even bigger fight. I left it alone.

"Trust me, I'll make it up to you … I just can't tonight."

"Are you chartering tomorrow?" she asked.

"Yeah, five a.m."

"That's early, even for you, Mr. Pickford." When she called me by my last name, I knew she was over our spat.

"Yup, tomorrow's going to be a busy day. Running across the harbor to Cape Haze Point first thing to catch bait, and client pick-up is at eight a.m., Ponce."

"Impressive," she said.

"What is?"

"You normally won't start your charter until after nine a.m."

"I know, but these particular clients pre-paid, and I need to cover all bases."

The conversation was going mediocre. I wasn't prepared for her to ask about my destination.

To end the call, I needed a slick segue. "Hey, Scupper is running toward the ramp, I've got to go. Call you tomorrow?"

"You better," she replied. The call ended on a positive note. Sara wasn't a complicated woman, and I liked that.

Now that the situation had been reconciled, I felt a subtle spring to my step.

In the house, with great luck, in my cooler, I found a cold beer positioned in a watery, ice mix. "Perfect."

After cracking down the tab, a small wave of iced steam rose from the can. I sat in comfort on the lanai, watching the dock through the narrow, overgrown ten-foot-wide path I had carved from the landscaping disarray. My yard was blanketed in palmetto bushes, overgrown sable palms, and sugar sand by the thousands of pounds which was home to many a fire ants' nest. Scupper pranced up and sat next to me. I sipped the beer.

The phone rang. It was Klinger!

Chapter Thirteen

Klinger Lee Nowell spoke in a deliberate tone, a forced intensity; his words were rushed and seemed rehearsed. I wanted to know how my old friend was dealing with the tragic incident that happened a few months back, maybe learn of his mental status, but I choked and mentioned the Brant situation and ended up explaining its entirety. It was good to hear his voice.

During our phone talk, Klinger protested my insistence that I could manage the situation alone. He argued that a mission like this was a two-man operation, and if I agreed, he would provide his unwavering help. He made me realize that taking the risk alone was unwise when he was willing and able to help. His tone suggested that every effort I made to convince him otherwise was pointless—same ol' Klinger. I finished the beer excitedly and drove to pick him up.

As I drove, I soaked in the Sunday night air, filling my lungs peacefully. There were no storms tonight, so the air was hot but light, not typical for this time of year. After pressing the clutch, I slid the truck into fifth gear and cruised at fifty-five miles per hour. After a few minutes, I came to the scene of the hit-and-run involving the owl, reminding me to call the Peace River Wildlife Center this week and check on the poor bird's fate.

Klinger's house was located in an area called the Ranchettes—a large parcel subdivision near interstate I-75. It sits on two acres of kid clutter and junk. His lawn business was obvious upon entering. A hydraulic, zero-turn commercial mower sat at the head of the dirt driveway along with mildewed kiddie toys falling upside-down. His five kids had clearly made their mark on his petite, manufactured house with a detached garage.

A scrawny silhouette stood in a garage-light penumbra, elbows tight to his ribs. Klinger wasn't known for his promptness—but there he was, standing, hands stuffed in jean shorts pockets. He wore a tight, dried blood-colored tank-top with short yellow circled armholes. On his head was a straw hat—same goatee, same tan feet. He loaded in, and we rode to the center of Port Charlotte, toward the warehouse.

Our greeting was short. There was no "Glad to see you-s" or "It's been a long time." No, not yet.

We hit US41 and Klinger broke the silence: "'Is goin' be crazy, man. Think he gonna play har' ball wit yah?"

"Planning on nothing other than that," I answered.

I was good to hear my friend's excitement after all this time. I'd missed his turbulent vibe for too long. Last time we were together, things didn't turn out so well. I again, for the time being, declined to mention anything related to the incident out at the Turtle Bay fish shack.

I said, "On the phone Mr. Northwood sounded like a man who didn't hear the word *no* very often."

"Once he sees 'at video yah mentioned, he ain't gonna 'ave no good choice but give up the loot, right?"

"That's the idea."

He grinned. "See, 'at's our ace up the sleeve, man. 'At video."

"Yeah, he made a point that I bring it with. He doesn't know anyone else is involved. Seems to think I'm solo on this, which is a good advantage."

"What 'appened to ol' Cliff-ereen-o?"

The decision not to involve Cliff any longer had been done subconsciously. I was planning to finish this ordeal alone, but then Klinger entered the situation. I didn't intentionally forego asking Cliff to accompany me. It just fell into place.

"Cliff has to open the deli tomorrow, so he's probably calling it a night." I didn't particularly feel good about the lie.

Klinger suggested, "I think we should make a'few copies and whatnot … of 'at video. *Juuust* in case."

I agreed and handed over my phone, allowing him to send the video to his phone through email.

"Whoa!" Klinger said as he watched the video. "Yah can't do 'at!"

"Unbelievable, right?"

"Dang, man." He shook his head in disgust. "People wit all the means think they entitled to all the gettin'."

"No doubt," I said. "Send a copy to my email address as well. Better to have a few copies."

Klinger laid both phones on his bony knees. "Right, 'at seems wise. One problem though, it says file too large for email, man."

"Are you serious, right now?"

"Yup, say it right 'ere … watch."

I lifted my eyes off the road for a spit second to view it. "Not good!"

"So, what w'gonna do now?" he asked.

The white lines in the middle of US41 were great for focus. I thought about the possibility of a plan B.

Klinger continued fumbling with my phone, attempting to send the video repeatedly, but the same result continued.

"Try this," I suggested. "See if you can load the video onto the memory card."

Klinger touched fast through different screens. He appeared to have it done. "Okay, I'm pre'y sure it's loaded up on 'is card now."

"Now take the card out and insert it into your phone."

Klinger flipped over the phone and removed the micro-memory card. He did the same on his phone.

"Got it?" I had little patience.

Klinger showed a slight smile. "So far *sooo* good, man."

"Are you Sure? A lot rides on this video…"

Klinger waited much longer than he needed to. "Lookin' like we good t'go."

"At last," I said relieved. "Something is going my way. So, you've got a copy now, too, right?"

"Look like it. Showin' under my videos." He played back the video. "Yup, is all 'ere, man."

"Good."

We passed Hooters and into the industrial park Cliff and I were at the previous night and parked in the same spot—the view of the warehouse unchanged.

"What time is the ol' meetin'?"

"Graham said ten o'clock."

Klinger noticed several parked vehicles. "See 'em cars?"

"Sure do. That's the place."

"Look like the whooole gang is 'ere,"

"Yeah, this is going to be interesting."

"Are yah walkin' in just like 'at … without the *Buff* for cover?"

"I guess so…"

Klinger finished a random thing on his phone and slid the phone onto the truck's dashboard. He peeked around while I sat and studied the warehouse. From the corner of my eye, a flicker of light, a pinprick spark, and then the soft sound of fire crackle. Klinger had lit a spliff and was puffing hard. Soon after, the unmistakable vapor of cannabis filled the cab.

I in no way would ever expect Klinger to relinquish cannabis, but under the current circumstances, I would think a little bit more discretion would be had. But I realized *it was* Klinger. I watched him take another pull.

"Smells delicious."

Before deciding whether to partake before the big meeting was a good idea or not, the joint was between my fingers, headed for my lips. The white smoke filled my lungs and stimulated a coughing fit. I fought it, eased an exhale, handing the offering back to Klinger, and then checked my watch: 9:40 p.m.

"It's getting close," I said.

"Sure is," Klinger said. "So, what yah gonna say in there anyhow?" He nodded toward the metal building. "Is there a plan?"

I sat a moment before answering. "There's *definitely* a plan. But it seemed to have slipped the mind." Suddenly, I wasn't so sure.

Klinger laughed. "'At cann'bis got yah mind boggled, huh?"

"Nah, I'm good, you?"

Klinger shook his head. "You beeetter get it together, man. From what yah told me, he meeeans *business.*"

"It's cool. I've got it." I glanced back at the warehouse, thought again, and said after a moment, "I'm not so sure I'm up to the task right now. We should probably reschedule … what do you think? Hooters is right … over there. Grab a beer?"

"Man, snap out it," Klinger said—then lifted off his seat briefly in excitement. "Get yah ass in gear 'en focus!"

My eyes went wide alongside Klinger's enthusiasm. "Hey, I've got an idea! *You* go in and say you're me?"

Klinger sat back. He first seemed at ease, but then his leg rocked back and forth with a nervous tick. He thought hard about it—a clench of jaw, a pulse of forehead vein, a tightening of brow muscles. He mustered up the courage and said, "I'll do it!"

I knew I could always count on Klinger. But seeing his stress, I couldn't let him do it. "Just playing around," I said. "This is my show."

Klinger took a deep breath.

"How much time have we got until ten?" I asked.

"Yah got…" His illuminous cell phone screen lit his face, "…five minutes."

I sat dumbfounded, clueless about how to handle it. I tried slapping myself in the face, jolting back any sense of levelheadedness. I then faced Klinger.

He was grinning. "Nice, feel better?"

"A little."

"W'ale, I should 'ope so," he said, and then went on: "Listen, man … yah need t'take a deeeeep breath." He led by example and waved in toward his chest.

I did what he said. "Hey, did you happen to bring your *Buff*?"

"Look ou'side, man." My inebriation was now fun for Klinger. "I's dark, dude."

"Worth a shot." I slouched and realized it had come down to the wire. I should've planned better, and apparently, I had to confront Graham without a disguise. Who did I think I was trying to blackmail a pro like Graham? I am sure he's been through this kind of thing dozens of times. Like I could compete with him? Then it came to me like an unexpected snook pop—the glovebox!

"Do me a favor?" I asked Klinger, who was re-weaving a piece of straw into his hat. "Open the glovebox, would you?"

Klinger agreed, and what slipped out and fell to the floor ... the *Beardo*.

"Hand that to me?"

Klinger's slanted eyebrow told me he wasn't amused by the idea. "Yah *ain't* gonna wear 'at, are yah?"

I placed it on my face. "Yup. It will disguise my face. It's perfect." Although the fake beard appeared ridiculous, it might work better than the *Buff*.

"Dude, no," he said.

I removed my visor and pulled the fake beard overtop my head and face. "How does it look?"

He sat back. "Hmmm. Like a guy tryin' t'conceal his dang identity ... 'at's what yah look 'ike, man."

"I think it will do just fine."

Not swayed, Klinger replied, "If yah say so, man."

A last-minute adjustment confirmed the fake beard to be quite disguising.

"Yah ready?" Klinger asked, as if a coach, leading me into a game.

I cracked the door. "Better now than never."

Klinger took my arm, spoke softly, "Know what yah aught'n do, man?"

"What's that?"

"Aught 'en record 'em. Get 'em awn tape."

"Really?"

"Oh, yeah—more ev'dence, the better."

I paused at Klinger's suggestion—it made perfect sense. If I could record Graham confessing, then it would be detrimental to his case.

My grin approached fast. "Interesting…"

"Yeah, buddy." He nodded. "Get 'em awn tape. Use your phone. He'll 'ave *no* clue."

I thought briefly, then affirmed, "I'll mull it over on the way."

"Oh-kay, I'm just gonna sit right 'ere and watch 'is truck—*pro*-tect it."

"Works for me," I answered. "Watch out for the cops, okay?" Somehow Klinger's initial offer to fill in as me, in some profound way, solidified our friendship even greater, and gave me an air of confidence.

My heart raced while I drew closer to the warehouse. The *Beardo* was disguising more than just my face; it also was masking the stabbing nervousness inside. Thinking of Klinger, I decided to record Graham and prepared my phone.

Moments later, I penetrated through the bushes framing the building's quaint parking lot, leading onto the asphalt. A light shone through the door and squared on the blacktop. None of the cars were occupied. I breathed one last deep breath before reaching for the door, but before I could grasp the knob, it swung open, and fixed in the doorway blocking the light, stood Graham—his tall silhouette, skinny and frail, obviously expecting my arrival. *Graham two ... Shamus zero*, I thought.

He wasted no time getting to the point—chin up, he said, "You must be...?"

I never gave him a name. "Captain ... you can call me Captain." *Not bad for a quick reply*, I thought.

He grinned suspiciously and said, "Over this way."

I followed him through the dark hallway leading out to a stained-cement warehouse floor, where several cars in white protective covers were parked, resembling a row of cocoons. To be exact, ten cars lined the belly of the warehouse. In the corner sat a tunnel hull flats boat of unknown make or model. It had a black painted engine cowling, and the center console was missing. Between the boat and the cars, a man swept the floor with a dustpan and broom.

Graham noticed me noticing the cars. "Those are for sale if you're interested."

If I was correct, those must be consignment inventory—vehicles left behind by customers. *Shady, but no harm in that*, I thought, continued following him across the wide-open floor. Fresh drywall scented the room as Graham strolled as though he were on a South American bleached-white sandy beach. A callous, empathetic-less man might walk the same way. In his head, he probably didn't have a care in the world.

Flip's voice sprung to mind. *"People gawn do what they gawn do."*

He led me into a cramped office near a window overlooking the warehouse floor. He slipped behind a narrow desk that belonged inside a 1980s secretarial office—wood, fake grain laminate sheets cut to size and glued overtop particle board. Fluorescent lighting made it irritating to see—one long tubular bulb, half-dead, flickered on and off. Numerous tacked notes and messages spread across the walls—names and addresses; some had pictures, others didn't. There was a hint of randomness that projected busyness. He saw my disguise and eyed it, as though impressed.

"I think we need to get the obvious out of the way," he said.

"Trust me, I'm not recording you." *Stupid*, I thought. *Dang cannabis!*

He smiled at the willingness I gave up such information. "Now, how can I be sure?"

"I have all I need," I said, cocky—a little too cocky.

"I'm sorry. I'm going to need some kind of proof. You've got to understand the prudence?"

"Of course, I understand, but proof?" I asked on offence.

"Yes." He eyed me head to toe. "Proof that this conversation will remain in this room, between us."

"How do I know *you're* not recording *me?*"

He frowned and realized the circular logic and said, "There's certain levels of secrecy I'm willing to give up, but right now I need you to do something for me."

"Which is?"

"You're a young man. Even wearing that fake beard, it's easy to see. The eyes, they say a lot."

"Oh, really?" I said. *Damn, this guy is good.*

"I wouldn't be far off in accusing you of having a cell phone, no?"

I accepted it and said, "Of course you wouldn't. Nearly everyone has them these days."

"Good, so it wouldn't be out of the question to assume yours is on your persons?" He eyed my shorts.

"That would be a safe assumption, yes."

"Good—then I'd like you to take it out."

"Out?"

"Yes, out. I'm not requesting much here, Captain. No confiscation or anything of that nature. Just take it out and set it on the desk."

My arms dangled to the side. I thought his request was reasonable, but then paranoia set in. I eased a muggy hand down my pocket. The screen was presenting the device's recording ability. Red recording icon flashing—no way would he miss it. Denying his request now would be an admission of guilt. I eased my finger to the power button, though it was a trigger during a duel, holding it steadily. There was no way to know whether the phone was off or not unless I removed it from my pocket.

Graham sat, gouty fingers interlocked behind his head, leaning, arching the squeaky chair to a tilt.

Fidgetiness and delay projected my obvious culpability. I peeked into the pocket. The screen seemed black, so with the least amount of nervous shaking, I removed it. Said, "Better yet, I'll just shut it off, okay?" Luckily, it had gone off, and then I flashed him the dark screen.

He nodded satisfactorily. "Appreciate that." His eyes then anchored to the flatness of the table. "Do you mind?"

I placed the phone down on the desk. "And your phone?" I asked.

"Mine? I left in the car—parked outside."

I said, "How can *I* be sure *you're* not hiding one to record me?"

He blinked. "You can't. This is my warehouse and there could be hidden cameras and microphones all over this place. Let that soak in for a moment…"

I stood and hoped that he was oblivious to the beads of sweat forming on my forehead. He was planting the idea in my head—of which I was sure.

I said, "So, I have given you all the proof I can, and you have zero to give me?"

"The proof is obvious."

"How so?"

He folded his hands and rested them onto the desk. "Why would I tape you?" he asked.

The question was dispiriting, and right in front of my eyes, he was lending me his experience. I sighed in defeat. The only leverage I had now was the video.

He didn't dwell, leaned back, and said, "So, you've got something for me?"

"And what would that be?"

He sighed. "So, we're going play this game, are we?"

I blinked in a loss of thought.

He went on, "I've heard a rumor that you have my son, Brant, recorded on some sort of video… Is that true?" He raised a chin toward the ceiling in a monstrous gloat.

"That's correct. I do have such a video, but where I'm from it's called cheating, and I'm not sure what you mean by 'got something for *you*.'"

"The video is irrelevant at this point," Mr. Northwood explained. "My son, he said he's viewed it and that's all that matters. The real question is … what do *you* want?"

"I want you to return the prizes and boat voucher to the rightful winners." I paused—continued, "Do you know that the people you cheated are locals and one of them is very sick? I mean *really* sick—bad liver." I wasn't attempting to guilt this man into returning the winnings—I was after his pure reaction—gauge his head.

He eased forward and opened a long drawer below his elbow. I tensed, squinted, and rose to my toes. I hadn't planned on a gunshot wound tonight. I tried to play cool while he lifted a half-full bottle of Maker's Mark and two cocktail glasses from the drawer.

"Drink? …Captain?" He splashed two shots into each glass.

I relaxed, accepted after a heavy-breathed exhale. After avoiding the fake beard hair, I sipped, trying to hide the fact my throat was on fire, but swallowing hard might have given that away.

Before Graham Northwood swallowed the shot, he swished it like mouthwash, shifting his wrinkled neck and Adam's apple. "Have you ever owned or ran a business, Captain?"

"As a matter of fact—" I caught myself before mentioning my charter business. "No, no I haven't."

"Then you know nothing about making the hard decisions, the ones that only serious businessmen must make."

I concurred.

He continued the speech, "I've ran a number of businesses … ones that required me to make certain kinds of decisions, which, frankly, I'm not proud of but, never-the-less, they had to be made." He took a nasally breath and went on, "Think of it this way: the needs of the many outweigh the needs of the few."

"So, by *many*, you mean your employees and *your* friends?"

"Well, in a sense, yes."

"This is exactly—"

He waved off my words and continued. "The people you speak of, the sick one, did they not have an equal chance to get an advantage at the tournament?"

Understanding the rhetorical question, I blinked at its stupidity.

He went on, "You've got to take chances to get ahead in this world. Understand?"

I said, "I must say you have an interesting viewpoint, but I think you're confused. This tournament is not business. These events are supposed to be friendly competition. The fact that they add expensive gifts, and the lure of cash, doesn't excuse the behavior of your son and his sidekick."

He shifted in his seat, to loosen muscles. "Very well, and that may be true. This warehouse ... the one we're in right now, I've had it for many years now. I use it for sort of an overflow kinda of storage. What I can't fit at my showroom in Ft. Myers, I leave here."

"So," I said, glancing around the room. "What exactly do you do anyway ... business-wise?"

"I own and operate a consignment business. Last time I checked we're up to around one hundred employees." He held the moment hostage, eyeing me, waiting for a response, but I gave nothing. "I was a young guy like you once, full of drive, ambition ... cared about the world. I started this business..." He peeked about. "...out of my parent's garage back in the seventies—from scratch. I had a friend who went off and joined the Army, and he asked me if I would sell his car for him, and upon the sale's completion, send him the money. I agreed of course. Sold the car alright, after showing it to about twenty people. Some called, made appointments, then never showed up, wasting my time—you know how it goes ... those sorts of things. When the car sold, I sent the money after taking a small cut. I put a lot of work getting the word out. Figured I deserved a little off the top. Since that point on, I've been doing it ever since. In fact..." He pointed his crooked finger at an old dollar bill tacked up on the wall. "This is the first dollar I earned—from my friend." He flicked the bill and finished, "I keep it as a reminder of how I got to where I am today."

"Impressive," I said sarcastically.

"It is. And all employees have health benefits and retirement plans—all paid for by acquiring a small advantage every now and again."

"So, the cash *and* the boat from the tournament will be invested by you, into your business, and to your employees? Not directly into *your* bank account?" Preparing for a sly response, I crossed my arms.

"Not exactly." He now realizing my expectations, squinted, and lightened the response. "I see that you're a passionate man, Captain... And I do believe that *you* believe you're doing the right thing here, but I see no reason that we can't work out some kind of agreement, no?"

I paused for effect. "I'm listening."

Before he could continue, a flushing sound from a door off to the side caught the room's attention. Both our heads turned. The door opened and out walked the man who had caterpillar eyebrows. The man waddled to a slim, ornate, green cornered chair. He sat, testing the integrity of the manufacturer's recommended weight limit.

Graham turned to the man. "Carl, this is Captain. He's the one I mentioned on the phone."

In the chair, Graham now spun to me. "Captain, this is Carl Bennet, he's a business partner of mine."

I about slipped and mentioned remembering him from the party but caught myself.

The man said nothing, kept on an unhappy, unsatisfied frown. The eyebrows on Carl were bushy and offensive. He had the same grumpy vibe from the party and wore a tight blue polo blouse and max-stretched gray slacks.

Graham noticed my detestation for him. "Carl and I go way back. Isn't that right, Carl?"

Carl nodded but said nothing.

Graham grinned and said to me. "He's not much of a talker."

"I noticed." I then thought back to the weigh-ins when Brant was led into the white tent next to the stage. The man sitting in the chair tucked in the corner of the cold room was indeed the same man who was in that tent. What they had been doing in the tent only raised more questions.

"So," Graham said, as though he'd sorted everything out. "You see there is nothing to be concerned about—"

I interrupted, "Well, I understand *you* believe that *you're* doing the noble thing by making the so-called "hard decisions" but taking what isn't rightfully yours is stealing. You didn't win the tournament honestly."

Graham mouth opened to speak.

I waved him off. "So, can you genuinely tell me, you'd have no problem facing the two men right now and telling them the story you just told me and expect them to understand? They'd maybe reply: 'Hey, no problem, man. Go ahead, take the prizes, we don't mind. It's cool. I want your employees to have a wonderful retirement plan?' Ridiculous…"

The shrewdness returned—a concurring smile had formed. "You would be surprised what they'd say…"

"What's that supposed to mean?"

"Okay, Mr. Captain, I'll level with you. What's really going on here is this: I've—"

I cut him off. I was charged up. Said, "I've read numerous articles on how most people in upper management, such as yourself, have a lack of empathy. It's practically a job requirement. How else can you do what you do?"

Carl sighed annoyingly.

"Is that so?" Mr. Northwood stood, frustrated, and faced out the window, peering out to the warehouse floor. His hands were fists inside his pockets. A reflection glared from the glass, presenting a youthful face, sending his complexion back twenty years. "Listen, Captain," he said. "I'd very much like to settle this tonight, once and for all. There's no reason to continue this any further. What I want to tell you is—"

I felt I was getting inside his head, so I hammered down my argument. "They walk among normal people every day. They have no idea what it means to feel empathy—don't know what it is and can't understand it … probably never will. Some people might call it sociopathic."

"Let me explain…"

I raised my hand, couldn't bear to listen to him lecture me about hard decisions. I didn't want to hear any more business advice from him. I said, "If you're not going to hand over the goods, then I'm done here." I felt the notion my threat wasn't as effective as I'd hoped, but I needed to stay in control.

"I—"

"That's enough," I said. "I'm turning you in."

"Let's not do anything irrational, son. We need to agree on something. I'm putting my trust in Brant and believing that the video he says you have is authentic, and it's no surprise I want it destroyed. Listen for a minute and I'll explain everything."

"I'm done listening." I made for the door, snatching the handle. "If it's not an admission of guilt, then I don't want to hear it."

He paused, letting out a breath through his nose, short and sharp, the kind meant to cool a fuse that was already burning. He didn't like the fact I attempted to control the situation. Said, "Let's come to an agreement, if nothing else. Will you at least let me offer one?"

Hearing the tall, bony man in gray dress shorts and a collared shirt again try to manipulate, made me defiant. There was only one outcome I wanted from this, and I decided I wasn't giving in, but would entertain his offering. "Okay, what do you have in mind?"

I focused in on his reflection. His mouth moved, then the words, "I'm willing to offer you five thousand dollars. The prize money was twenty-five grand. You take five of that and I watch as you destroy the video."

"Thought you said the video was irrelevant?"

"Indeed, I did. It seems the situation has changed, and I can sense you're not in a listening mood, and I'm a busy man and have little time … or patience for this sort of insulting."

"You should have thought things through before deciding to involve yourself in this."

He nodded and his tone changed to that of a tired old man. "Very well," he said, and poured another two shots of Maker's Mark.

Before answering, or contributing more to the conversation, I ran through other options. One would be to turn Brant and his dad into the tournament officials and let them deal with it, but I'm no rat, so that's only an idle threat. Another option would be to threaten by way of force. I liked the latter of the two, but that could create more trouble for me. I decided letting Graham squirm for a little while longer was the appropriate step—punishment.

I told the man, "Well, since things have changed, I'd have to mow it over for a little while."

"Good grief…" he said. The man eased over, and onto a scratch pad scribbled something and handed it to me. His mouth was dry, tacky from the liquor. "Here, take this."

I accepted the paper and read a cell phone number written in neat, sharp penmanship. I then placed it inside my pocket, said nothing. The *Beardo* had begun to itch, and there was an overwhelming urge to scratch it. I picked up my phone, took the shot of liquor, and leaned back toward the doorway.

Carl kept still and continued scrolling the screen of a cell phone.

Graham led me through the warehouse floor and now stepped heavily and tiresomely down the short hallway. He opened the metal door, and I stepped out.

"Give me a call when you decide what to do," he said. "I'm offering you this courtesy, and I'd appreciate the same in return. Next time we talk, you may not like what I have to say."

The door shut and the 'clack' of the deadbolt spoke for him.

****

I headed for my truck, stepping through the bush adjacent to the street when I noticed something disturbing. The truck was gone. "Shit," I whispered. "Where did you go, Klinger?"

Both directions were empty. Instincts led me toward the sound of US41. I skipped, putting distance between the warehouse and myself, and decided on leaving the *Beardo* on until reaching US41. After each small side street, I searched for my truck. A quarter mile later, down the final side street, there was a flash of headlights. The vehicle's stance said volumes, the size, the tires, all helped determine its make and model. I approached the truck with caution. Klinger was sitting behind the wheel pressed against the driver's windshield. I sighed in relief.

Upon opening the passenger door, the smell of stale cannabis saturated the air inside the cab.

"What happened?" I asked.

Klinger said in a tremulous croak, "Cops, man. 'Ad nooo choice."

I checked behind us. "Let's get out of here."

Klinger fired up the truck, gripped the manual gear shifter, and after hard-grinding the gears, chaotically found first gear.

I asked, "Did they ask you to move ... the cops?"

"No, but af'er a'second drive by, I decided I better get the heck outa 'ere."

"Good move," I said.

We hit US41 and headed south. Klinger drove safe—speed good, slowly adjusting to the manual transmission.

"Where to?" he said.

"Not sure at the moment," I said, checking to see if we had a tail. "Let's just keep on heading south."

A red stoplight approached, and Klinger focused on downshifting.

"Easy…" I said. "I thought you knew how to drive manual? You usually back the truck down the ramp   fine."

 "I got it … like ridin' a bike."

At a red light, I plucked out my cell and dialed Donny Elrod. After five rings, he picked up.

A groggy, hoarse voice uttered, "This better be good!"

"Donny, it's Shamus," I said through the phone.

"I know it's you. I have caller ID, dumbass."

"You're right, you're right. Did I wake you?"

"Hell yeah, you woke me. It's ten-thirty."

"I know, I'm sorry for that, but I need a second to talk."

"I gotta get some sleep. My shift starts at three a.m."

"I know. This should only take a second."

"Okay, fine," he said. "What is it?"

"Remember the tournament yesterday? Our little conversation?"

"Oh, yeah. How'd that go? I been meanin' to call you and find out."

"Well … let's just say it went the way I thought it would—with one little snag…"

"So, you're sayin' that you caught those guys? What's his name, Brant? He's the doofy, blond one?"

"Yes, we did. Cliff and me, and we have it on tape."

"Video?" he asked.

"Oh yeah," I said, smiling into the phone.

Now his voice became less sleepy. "Oh, I gotta see this."

I tried to bait him in. "Yup, caught them red-handed."

"Nice!" he replied.

"Got the video right here, on my phone."

He asked, "Can you email it to me?"

I adjusted the phone and said to Klinger, who was concentrating on driving, "Um—not right now."

"What's your twenty?" he asked.

"Right now, I'm headed down US41, toward Punta Gorda."

"Right, right ... I'll meet you in ten minutes. You know the spot."

He ended the call.

Chapter Fourteen

"**D**o me a favor?" I asked Klinger.

"Sure, what's 'at?"

"Pull into the parking area next to the Punta Gorda bridge for a minute. Live Oak Park."

"Wus 'at Donny? On the phone?"

"Yeah, I want to run a few things by him."

"How'd the meetin' with Graham go?" he finally asked.

"It went kinda strange."

"Strange?" he asked.

"Yeah, he tried to buy me out."

Klinger merged into a turning lane, crossed US41, and rolled the Toyota into the gravel-filled parking lot next to the bridge.

"Are yah serious, Shamus?"

"As a poached snook."

"I can't b'lieve it, man. Are yah sure? Ma'be yah heard wrong … yah know, cause of the cannabis and whatnot. Sometimes it disrupts hearin'."

"Oooh-no," I said. "I know exactly what I heard in there. The old man explained it all. Says that he's doing the 'greater good'—quoted Spock and tried laying down his life story about how he started the business in his garage and 'You gotta make hard decisions to make it in this world'… blah blah blah."

"Wow, 'at's nuts, man.," Klinger pulled into a random spot and shut off the engine. "So, when did he try en' buy yah off?"

"At the end. I couldn't listen to him ramble on anymore. He became frustrated and offered the cash to me. He's a smooth talker, that's for sure."

Klinger still had the same anxious fluttering in his voice. "How much he offer us?" He paused, biting a nail. "I mean, you. Was it all cash?"

"Yes, and it was five thousand."

"Daaang," Klinger replied and faced forward.

"Yeah, the nerve."

"Did yah show 'em the video?"

"Nope, he said five thousand and he insists on watching me destroy it."

"Man, you shou'd 'ave just destroyed the one awn your phone, taken his money. We still 'ave copies … maybe use 'em f'more money … yah know, as leve'age or sumthin?"

"No, absolutely not! One way or another, this is ending—tonight."

"I sup'ose you're right," my friend said, lowering his chest as his anxious voice yielded to acceptance.

We sat a few seconds in cold silence. I had to know how Klinger was doing after the nightmare at the fish shack but didn't want to pressure him. I knew what he had been through, and the stress that day must have caused him. I felt the awkwardness beginning to set in, so I asked, "So, how you been? I mean how *have* things been since … you know…"

Klinger answered as though he'd been ready to talk for a while. "W'ale … I ain't over it b'any means."

I nodded in agreement. "Gotcha. No reason you should be." My friend and I witnessed a murder several months back. His connection to the victim was much closer than mine.

Klinger's leg began to shake. "Yeeup, Mandy's got m'goin' to a shrink," he said. "Can ya'believe 'at?"

I nodded again in agreement that Mandy, his wife, was taking good care of him. "That might not be a bad thing—talk it out."

"I'm only goin' 'cause she wants me to. Mandy says I've been screamin' out loud in m'sleep … wakes'er up, and sometimes the kids. She recorded it, en'sure enough, i's true. Havin' nigh'mares almost eeevery night… Doc think's it's the ol' P-T-S-D."

I tried to sound consoling. "Well, you did go through a traumatic experience."

"I's bad. The other day, the mailman rang the dang doorbell and I 'bout jumped off the couch." He began to tap his knee nervously. "My heart was racin' and whatnot … i's an awful feelin', Shamus, awful."

I had never questioned the reality or the authenticity of Posttraumatic Stress Disorder. The human mind was a fragile thing, if not the most fragile of things—maybe even more so than life. It doesn't take much to knock the nervous system off track.

"Any meds…?"

"Yeah, she gi'me the usual … Xanax—but I'll tell yah, it makes m'like a zombie. All I wanna do is sleep, so I stopped takin' it."

"There's got to be something else that you could benefit from."

"There is." He grinned. "Cannabis."

I had to agree. Cannabis was extremely beneficial when it came to relieving anxiety.

"I saw Flip yesterday," I said. "He's back in town."

"Back?" he said, grabbing his chin. "Didn't know he w'gone."

"Yup. After the incident, he disappeared as well."

"Oh, man," he said, cracking a slight smirk. "I need go over 'en see 'em."

"That might be a good healing technique."

A flicker of two light beams shot across the parking lot. It was Donny's vehicle bouncing up and down, entering the stony road. He parked beside my truck.

"Let m'guess… Yah gonna run this brib'ry thing by Donny?"

"Pretty much, yeah," I answered.

Donny exited the car wearing black boots and a white bathrobe looking like a large snowman.

I greeted him. "I'm sorry for waking you, just—"

A smile cut me off. "It's fine—you'll just owe me two fishing trips."

I noticed the choice of clothing and teased, "What? You couldn't put on a pair of pants for me?"

"Listen, buddy. You got me out of bed for this, so this is what you get."

He and Klinger re-acquainted with the usual "How you been" routine, and Donny asked to see the video.

"Wow," he said, after reviewing just part of the five-minute recording. "I can't believe it, right out in the open like that." Donny watched the small screen, eyes wide. "These two are crazy."

I lowered the phone. "Amazing, right?"

"Dumb is a'better word," Klinger said.

"I can't believe you caught them! What did you two do?" Donny asked. "Follow them all day?"

"That's exactly what we did … from mangrove bush to mangrove bush, then back to the dock. We almost lost them after weigh-ins."

"Wow, Shamus, you don't let anything go, do you?"

"Not like this I don't." My satisfaction was obvious.

"So, you're turning them in, right?" Donny asked. "Teach these two a lesson?"

"I lead them to believe that, but…"

Donny face turned skeptical. "But what?"

"I'm *no* rat," I said, glancing around. "And it's also gotten a bit more complicated. There's just one more detail I want to discuss…"

Donny's eyes lit up and his tone went giddy. "Oooh, okay. Well, lay it on me."

After running through the entire day from start to finish, and the meeting, Donny's anger was clear. He lived with a normally quiet, gentle temperament. Being such a big individual at six-foot-two and wide as semi-truck, he kept a calm demeanor on the surface, so as not to intimidate people.

"Crazy, right?" I said.

Donny remained silent, rubbing his bald head like a crystal ball.

I said, "And I found a bottle of pills in his bathroom that now seems more interesting."

"Oh yeah? What kind of pills?"

"*Propranolol.*"

"What's that for?"

"I think it's to control heart rate."

"Really?"

"Yes, like the kind you'd want to have if you needed to pass a certain test…"

Donny stomped his boot. "The lie detector!"

I said nothing and let the situation soak in.

While yawning, Klinger turned to a fisherman prancing up the bridge-protected sidewalk, carrying a fishing rod and bait pail. Overnight fishermen now began to line the bridge, pushing large-wheeled, sand-friendly carts—buckets, tackle boxes, and long dip-nets loaded heavy. People who were happier fishing evenings were now leaving, like the changing of a shift.

"Those sons of bitches!" Donny blurted, then shook his head. "That's what's wrong with these dang tournaments, people are going to cheat, one way or another—its human design not to play fair. By-catch, I guess…"

"Noooo *doubt,*" Klinger added.

"I mean—" Donny began intently.

I placed a hand on Donny's shoulder. "Relax, man. I don't want you blowing a gasket on me, and I sure don't want to have to carry your big ass to the hospital."

"I know, I know…"

"M'either, man," Klinger said late.

Light from the next-door gas station glistened off Donny's head. "So, are you going to take the cash?" he asked.

"Good question," I answered. "I'm not sure."

Klinger said, "I say take the cash, man."

"I think I probably would if the prizes weren't stolen from Randy and his sick father. That's royally messed up."

Donny's concern increased. "I agree, but are yah ready to compete with this guy Graham? He doesn't seem like the type to get pushed around."

"I agree," Klinger chimed.

"I know, but something has to be done," I said to both my friends. "*This* can't go unpunished."

Donny lowered his voice. "Shamus, I know how passionate you are about these things, but this might be too much. I know you were looking for the big score here, but these ain't the guys. They ain't worth it. Toss 'em back."

"I agree, man," Klinger said. "Toss 'em back."

"Whose side are you on anyway?" I asked Klinger. "Earlier, you were all gung-ho."

"I'ma awn your side, man, but I'd like to *not* 'ave this follow us," he paused to correct. "I mean *you* 'round. Yah know what I mean, right?"

"I understand your concern, really I do, but these things don't get better unless people like us step up and takes a risk, man."

Donny said, "Hey, even though Graham and Brand aren't quite your cup of tea, they at least won one back for the local guy. That's gotta earn them some points, right?"

"I hate you…"

All three of us breathed deep breaths and reflected. Donny again rubbed his head.

Klinger kicked a few loose pebbles and stubbed his toe. "Ouch, crap, dang-it." He stole a glance down the bridge at the night fishermen.

Donny broke the silence with, "You need to just take it, the money, and run. You can give it to the sick second-place team or do whatever with it."

Klinger agreed, checking his exposed toes.

I explained to Donny the release boat situation.

He laughed. "You didn't get in line?"

"Hell no, man!"

"I'm kidding, really," he said. "These tourneys breed bad behavior all around, I guess."

A pocket of cool air blew off from the water, gusting across us three. Klinger appeared drowsy, yawning nonstop. Donny stood in his bathrobe checking his watch, and I safely assumed the meeting was adjourned.

"Listen, Shamus," Donny said, "You know I've got your back, but this time I'm advisin' you. Take the money. No reason to drag it out. You busted them and they know it. No need to take it further."

In some way, both Klinger and Donny were genuine. Why *should* this drag any further? I'd walk away a couple thousand dollars heavier—maybe more, and then give it to Randy and Pete. And I'd likely never have my identity compromised. In all ways, Cliff was in the clear, too

The humid night triggered my sweat glands, exuding a thin film of sweat across most of my body. I thought of calling Sara to ask if she'd meet me in the shower in thirty minutes. The thought was motivation to forget the whole deal.

"Whudya say?" asked Donny.

"I guess I'll call it a night"

"Good."

"For now…"

"Listen to me." His voice became humorless. "Go home, have a beer, and get some sleep—then tomorrow call me and we'll talk, okay?"

"Agreed," I said for Donny's benefit. Truth is, I won't sleep tonight. With a possible shower date, plus an early morning charter, sleep was unlikely.

Klinger eased toward the truck's passenger side, insinuating who was driving home.

Donny said, "Okay, bud. Call me in the morning and we'll talk."

"Will do," I replied.

The ridiculous humidity was why I reached behind the seat for something to wipe off the sweat. My hand found the T-shirt from the Peace River Wildlife Center. I studied it.

"Whatever did happen to the owl?" I mumbled. Which then reminded me of the red Colorado pickup, and the driver who'd fled the scene. "Karma's going to get him…" As though a firework exploded in my head, the license plate number—*WSH1FSHN!* Donny could search up the plate number using his connections, get a bead on who this guy was.

As Donny pulled away, I swept in behind and flickered my high beams. His brakes sent beams of red light into the Tacoma's cab.

"Wha's up, man?" Klinger asked.

"I need to ask Donny one more thing."

I raced out of the truck and jogged up to Donny's vehicle.

He anticipated the arrival, motoring down the window. "What's up? Everything okay?"

"Yes, everything is fine," I answered. "Can you do me one quick favor?"

"Um … depends," he said.

"Something's been bugging me."

He snorted. "What's new…"

"Can you look one more thing up for me, on your little computer gizmo there?"

His teeth grinded. "Shamus, yah gonna get me so busted for this."

"One quick thing?"

"Jesus, okay, fine. What is it?"

"Can you search license plates?"

Donny peeked at me, half-smirking. "Are you kidding? 'Course I can."

I read the letters *W-S-H-1-F-S-H-N* to Donny, letter for letter. He didn't ask why I requested the information.

"Here you go."

"Find something?"

"Yup—registered to a guy by the name of Tyler Christianson, of Port Charlotte, Florida."

"Cool, thanks. Is there a picture?" I asked and then ran the name through my head over and over: *Tyler Christianson ... T-y-l-e-r Christian-son.* It didn't jog up a memory.

"Here you go," Donny said, adjusting the blinding bright laptop screen.

What I saw was truly shocking. I'd come to know the man quite well over the last forty-eight hours. It was almost too perfect. The man on the screen was the same man Cliff and I had secretly videotaped. Brant's sidekick.

In a clear hurry, Donny asked, "Got it?"

I'd come this far, so figured I'd push my luck. "Yeah, but hey ... there wouldn't be a phone number would there, associated with the picture?"

"Hang on." He clicked away and scrolled through the page, searching as though the quicker he found the requested information, the quicker he'd be back in his bed.

"I owe you big-time," I said.

"You got that right, bud."

"Really, let me know next time you and Brenda have a day off. Charter fishing on me."

"Don't worry, I will," he replied.

I wrote the number down on the same scratch paper Graham had written his number. I said goodbye to Donny and headed back to my truck. Klinger was inside, fast asleep. When I started the truck, my friend awoke.

"What's 'at all about?"

Before answering, I pondered whether Klinger would benefit from the newly acquired data.

"Had to see if he's available next week … to redeem this favor I owe him." An obvious lie, but Klinger's tiredness attributed to him leaving it alone.

Before Klinger left the cab, he told me how good it was to catch up, and how he thought he might give the medication another try.

Now alone in his driveway, I began to mull about the owl and felt it needed more justice. Something in my gut said to call the number Donny gave me. At the very least, I needed to check the legitimacy of it. So, I stayed put in Klinger's driveway and made the call.

It rang three times. A man answered. I hung up.

It was a big misstep to call from my personal cell. "Shit," I muttered. "Now, this guy has my number." Technology allows caller ID to be available standard on every phone plan; the chances were slim he hadn't recorded it. I remained still and waited—nothing—no callback. I decided to head home but managed just a mile when the phone rang back. It was Tyler's number.

The cell continued ringing another five rings and then fell silent. I waited for the vibration of a received voicemail, but none. Then it rang again. I breathed deep and answered, "Hello," in a piss-poorly disguised voice.

"Hello?" said the man on the other end. "Someone call me from this number?"

I figured at this point, no reason to lie. "Tyler?"

"Yes, it is," he answered.

"I think we need to talk."

"Captain?"

How did he know that name? Then I thought, Graham must have gotten word out as soon as our meeting had ended.

"Hello?" he said.

I held the phone out from my ear momentarily in shock.

"Let's meet," the voice rejoined again, speaking in a hasty tone.

Thoughtless, I blurted out a location. "Gilchrest Park ... I assume you know it?"

"Yes. On my way," he said—then the line went dead.

Five minutes later, I was there and extended a stride toward the fishing pier, but first snatched the *Beardo*—just in case.

At the first planks of the pier, a cool breeze flushed from the harbor. The winds had eased since the day before, their constant plying now just light as a breath. Moonlight pooled along the seawall, where clusters of people gathered in quiet silhouettes. I snuck to the middle of the pier for a better vantage point to the parking lot. The moon beamed excellent light, allowing first-rate visibility. I chose a spot that aligned my sight to both parking lot entrances—the main one, and a side entrance near the tennis courts. Rows of historical houses lined the broken cobblestone street, bestowing light upon parts of the old road, so the flashy red Colorado should be easy to spot.

Anticipating the meeting put me on edge. I was going in blind and impetuous, and far removed from my comfort zone. I stood alert and checked my watch. It had been ten minutes. I peeked around, and from the corner of an eye, spied a rugged truck contour barreling between two old white lines, slamming on brakes, bordering on a skid. The truck settled below a parking lot light—the red Colorado.

I stared, wickedly tense. Not right away did anyone exit. Moments later, the door opened, and someone's leg appeared. From my current distance, I couldn't perceive faces, just body shapes, and maybe heights. The person glanced around searching for someone— me.

I began the short walk off the pier, toddling toward the seawall. I stuffed the *Beardo* down my pocket, left the concrete path, aimed for the parking lot, and hit a short dirt path through the St. Augustine grass, dodging the dead, low hanging branches of a cabbage palm.

I zeroed in on the truck—then something happened. The passenger door opened, illuminating the cab, revealing a second person. "Perfect—he brought Brant," I whispered to the bark of a tall palm. I wasn't prepared to deal with Brant's unbridled ignorance. I'd rather talk to a toddler; at least they had the ability to reason. Tyler, on the other hand, was my last shot left for compassion. But his decision to bring Brant as backup didn't say much about his character.

Then I grew paranoid, and if Graham had indeed informed them about our recent meeting, have they been sent to take me out? "Crap, snap out of it!" I mumbled.

Rethinking my decisions surfaced a level of wariness I'd never felt before. It wasn't too late to hightail it out of here, head to the house, meet Sara in the shower, forget all of this. Something inside me wouldn't allow digression.

My back was pressed firmly against the uneven bark of a palm tree as I faced up to the night sky and saw the faintest glimpse of stars through the surrounding ambient light. All the decisions I'd made so far had led me to this point. A fleeting thought of recording Tyler sprang to mind. I laughed the idea out of my head.

I snuck a peek around the palm. Tyler was glancing about, attempting to see through the parking light's penumbra. He stepped to the edge to check the shadows of the sable palms. Inside the truck, Brant remained still.

"Screw it." I broke free from the palm, a steadfast tramp toward the parking lot light under which Tyler stood one hundred feet away. Because of the unforeseen added body, I went for the *Beardo* and placed it on my face. It went on, but it was impossible to measure the coverage. I worried no more as I neared the truck. Tyler saw me walking toward him, stiffened, then bowed up, to present himself as tough. He tapped on the driver's door window, notifying the passenger of my arrival.

I whispered, "Here goes nothing. If I get shot, I get shot."

I ambled into the light. Tyler remained in a defensive position; wore khaki shorts, a baseball jersey, and a Tampa Bay Devil Rays hat laid on backwards. His neck was missing, and his head sat on shoulders wrapped in bulging traps.

He noticed my guard.

"Relax," I said in a calm manner, as if talking to a vicious dog.

"No problem here," he responded. "Are you … Captain?"

I nodded and asked my own question. "Tyler?"

His eyes were squinted—cautious. "I see you felt the need to wear a disguise," he noted.

"Sometimes you've gotta use the tools that you're given," I replied. "But I wouldn't worry about that right now. We need to have a talk."

"That's why we're here, isn't it?"

"Yes, and first things first, I need you to call the Peace River Wildlife Center and check on the owl that you hit, and also make a donation, and I better see you volunteering immediately. I want to see that red Colorado parked there every day for two weeks." I needed to take control first.

His brows raised and his eyes opened wide. "How did you know about that?"

I didn't answer yet focused on the passenger seat. The man didn't move, and the dark interior disclosed a dull silhouette. Thoughts of getting shot through the windshield passed, and I decided to get a bead on Tyler's loyalty to Graham, asked, "What's the deal with the tournament winnings? Are you getting a piece of the action?"

His chin raised. "Nope."

"No? That's not fair, now is it?"

He sensed my inclination and ignored the question, asking his own. "What is it that *you* want out of this? Are you thinking about turning all of us in? I mean—really?"

"That's the plan, if you don't comply."

"Comply?"

"Simple," I said, staring directly in his eyes. "Give all the proceeds to the team you cheated out."

"That it?" he said on the verge of a laugh.

"Yes."

He faltered aside, leaned his back on the car's driver-side rear door, and crossed his arms. He sensed victory. "How did you get that video anyway?"

"I took it," I told him. "And how did *you* find out about it?"

"How do you think? Brant told me. He said you confronted him in the bathroom at Hooters. Slick move."

"Yeah, your friend, Brant … he's umm…" I lowered my voice and glanced toward the passenger seat. "…he's a meathead."

"He's not that bad once you get to know him."

My reply was skeptical. "If you say so."

"So, are you going to let me see this video that everyone seems to be so concerned about?"

"Maybe—but I must warn you, I have copies."

"*Of course*, you do," he replied.

Just as I reached down my pocket, to fetch the phone where the video was stored, the Colorado's cab light flickered on. The passenger door was now ajar. *Great, here we go,* I thought.

I pulled the phone out, sifted through data, and retrieved the video. As I did it, from my peripherals, movement stepped ahead of the truck and slid in beside Tyler.

The man said to his friend, "We need more *beer.*"

As odd a thing that was to say, I fought to look. To my surprise thought, the man standing next to Tyler wasn't Brant at all, it was Randy.

Chapter Fifteen

y first reaction was gut, to run like hell, but I didn't, and with my head down, I pretended to search my phone.

I stared at the phone in complete confusion as my heart rate spiked. Was this some kind of joke? If these two were friends, then that meant Brant and Randy were friends too, or at the very least acquaintances.

"We'll get more beers on the way back to the house," Tyler said to his belligerent friend.

"Fine," Randy answered, staggering in place.

Most human beings can sense when they're being watched. I delayed no more and faced Tyler, who had been eyeing me the entire time.

"Surprised?" he said.

Feelings of overwhelming defeat coursed through my brain and humility got the best of me. I was frustrated and slid the phone down my pocket, turned, and trudged away.

"Hey! Where yah goin?" Tyler yelled.

I didn't react as I kept on pace.

He added, "Take the money!"

Chills blanketed my body. I spun around and stomped back under the light.

"Take the money?" I asked, offended. "So, if I understand correctly, you're all in on this?"

"Listen, friend," Randy said as he struggled with balance. "We understand where yah comin' from but—" He tried placing a compassionate hand on my shoulder.

I swayed back to avoid it. "Easy, bud." I tried concealing my voice in hopes that the drunken kid wouldn't recognize it—and at his current state of intoxication, unlikely.

Tyler grabbed his friend's arm and pulled him back. "Chill, okay?"

Randy leaned on the car.

"Listen, man," Tyler said to me. "I know why you're here."

"You do?"

He nodded.

I said, "Please explain because I'm not so sure I know why *I'm* here."

"You wanted this meeting so you could try and talk me into giving up the tournament winnings ... let's stop the games."

"Agreed," I replied, residing in brutal humility.

Randy's phone suddenly rang. His inebriated mind and clumsy hands answered it. "'Ellow!" he said, then stumbled to the passenger side of the Colorado, got in, and continued his conversation.

"Randy?" Tyler said to me, looking through the windshield, watching his friend plop into the seat. "We go *way* back."

I replied carefully, concealing what had happened on the West Wall: "Seems like a good kid."

Tyler reached into his pocket, slung out a pack of smokes, slid one to his lips, and lit it. He pulled heavily, indicating the conversation was about to get serious. "He's a good dude. You know his father's sick? He blew out the smoke. "Right?"

This question, like storm surge, flooded humiliation into me. "I do, yes."

"Well, I've known Randy and his dad for twenty years. We went through school together, starting in kindergarten."

I let him continue.

"I've watched his dad grow sicker and sicker throughout the years," he explained. "They've been through all kinds of treatment options … nothing's helped."

"So, you're saying this whole thing was planned by Randy?"

"No, I'm not saying that at all. I'm saying that he came to me and asked if I thought it was possible to rig the upcoming redfish tournament so he and his dad could win first place."

"And you agreed?"

"No, not at first. But after thinking about it for a few days, he mentioned his dad's medical bills were piling up. That got me wondering."

After hearing that, I just shook my head and let him talk.

"I didn't at first think it was possible, but after speaking to Brant about it, over many beers, it started to sound doable. I mean, you know teams have been cheating on those tournaments for years … let's not kid ourselves."

The more Tyler explained, the more he made sense. "Sure," I said.

"At first, I thought it was going to be impossible, and I wasn't going to participate. But then Brant's dad, Graham—who you've met—caught wind of it and said he could help. That he had "connections." Honestly, I think he wanted in on the plan to stroke his ego, nothing more, but he does have connections, so we all talked it out. The plan started slow but soon came together and everything fit in place—" He paused, peeked around, and continued, "Except *you*, of course. That, we didn't plan on."

By-catch, I thought. "How could you? There is always an element of risk when taking on a plan like that."

"Of course, there is," he said. "You also can understand why we did it, right? I'm sure you're just as frustrated as us … watching these out-of-town teams come into our town, shred up the water, and win these local tournaments, taking the winnings right out from under our noses, no?"

"I agree with that, but on occasion locals do win a tournament or two."

"That might be the case, but under the circumstances we just wanted to make sure, or at least *give* ourselves the *best* chance at winning."

I said, "So, I'm assuming Randy and his dad pulled their redfish from the same pen you and Brant did? That's why they came in second?"

"Pretty much," he answered. "They picked up their redfish before us. Randy phoned from the water and said his dad wasn't feeling well, so they went to the pens first."

This detail was something I wanted to ask, but he'd answered it for me. Cliff and I encountered Randy and Pete before we videotaped Brant and Tyler, and I remember Randy saying that they had a "couple nice ones to weigh in" and were visible in their live well.

"I see," I said. "It was just a matter of who picked the biggest fish, ultimately deciding who would win?"

"Exactly—could have been them. Just so happened that we picked the bigger two fish is all. I'm assuming you were at weigh-ins? It was *very* close. We just needed to guarantee victory."

"I see…"

"We just wanted to make sure *one* of us would win … no matter what."

I said, "Makes sense—both take the biggest fish and go from there."

"Brant and I just got lucky is all." He sensed my eagerness to interrupt but held up a hand to finish. "It didn't matter who won the tournament. The money and prizes are going to Pete's care. That, you can take to the bank."

"Really?"

"It's okay if you don't believe me, but it's all true—every last word."

"If you say so. You guys set the pens?"

"If you must know, the whole *pen* idea was Brant's, if you can believe it. I just wanted to leave the seine net out—"

"What?" I interrupted.

He flicked his cigarette out into the parking lot. It hit the ground, spreading the cherry into pieces. "Listen, it went down like this. We went out Thursday before the tournament and set up a seine net across Oyster Creek where you taped us. The next day, Friday, we checked the net mid-day and sorted out the biggest slot size reds we could. We only lost one or two, and let me tell yah, there were about two dozen oversized fish … I mean big bulls. We brought the best four fish to the pens and tossed chunks of cut bait inside and that was it. Come to find out from Randy that the reds remained alive and healthy, so it was just a matter of going and picking them out."

"Incredible… And the pens?" I asked.

"Gone—next morning. Following the tournament, early, we collected both fifty-five-gallon blue barrels."

"How did you get those obvious fish pens to the boat ramp?"

"We went out before first light—covered them in tarps," answered the kid standing in front of me, a composed explanation, though telling his buddies a fishing story. "And we didn't go back to the boat ramp, we off-loaded them at Brant's parents' house, in Punta Gorda Iles. Then I took them back to my house, off Burnt Store Road."

The owl! I thought.

As the story shaped in my head, I had to give them credit. The plan did end up working—except for me of course. "I see. So, that's that, huh? What about the boat voucher?"

"Graham's going to buy that from us for a quick buck, then he'll sell it at his consignment shop, that way Pete won't be waiting for cash."

I wanted to hate this kid but couldn't. Knowing the full scope of what these two had done would now make me question the legitimacy of every tournament from now on, even more than I already did. I didn't want to leave any holes. "What are these 'connections' that Graham said he had?"

He lowered his chin and broke eye contact. "I'm not sure I can tell you that one."

"Why not?" I asked. "You've basically told me the whole story. Why leave out this small detail?"

"I wish I could—but the answer to that question might not be a 'small detail.'"

"You're not *afraid* of Graham, are you?"

"No, no, nothing like that. Graham and I are cool. It's just a respect thing. If you really want to know the answer to that question, just ask him. He'll probably tell you."

"How long after I left the meeting did he call you?"

"Not long. When he called me, he said you had just left and that you're a pain-in-the-ass."

"Can you blame me?"

"I guess not."

I said, "Graham, he's a smart man, I'm surprised he involved himself in this."

"He has his reasons, I'm sure. So, knowing all this, are you still going to turn everyone in?"

"I'm not sure yet. I'll have to mull it over some more."

"If you say so," he replied, frustrated—then muttered, "Graham said you'd be difficult…"

"Say what?"

"Nothing," he replied and turned to leave. "Just take the money. Graham was banking on you taking it after you two had your meeting, but you seemed to be unsure."

"So, you're here to persuade me into taking it? Maybe give me a sob story?"

"Technically, you called me for the meeting, but I'm not going to lie and say that Graham didn't have a plan B."

"Figures," I mumbled.

Tyler asked, referring to the fake beard, and now thinking we're friends: "Is that thing hot?"

"It is, so I'm going to go think this out."

"Okay … but be quick about it. Pete doesn't have much time left." He had compassion in his voice. I hated myself for believing him.

With that, I scurried through the park, passed palm trees, returning to the edge of the pier. The air had dampened, and mist rose from small patches of grass. I walked the pier, needed a minute to regroup my thoughts and calm the maddening humility.

Chapter Sixteen

The next morning arrived after a sleepless, humility-filled night, contemplating certain situational aspects. Scupper remained at my side the entire night.

As I wiped the sleep from my eyes aboard my skiff, Spinner led me out of the basin as usual but swam back to feed on the rotating circles of mullet. Breathing in the crisp, pre-dawn air, I slammed the throttle and charged across Charlotte Harbor. There were no signs of a sea breeze, and the distance clouds were soft, fluffy, white balls of cotton suspended in midair.

I continued in search of bait conducive to large predatory fish that would facilitate my clients' best chance of catching the snook of a lifetime. Having pre-paid a healthy tip, obligation converted to motivation. After I located, caught, and filled the baitwell with magnificent-sized greenbacks, I gathered up the clients at Ponce de Leon Park.

I set up the two men in a deep channel at Bull Bay's northern rim. It was a slow start, the kind that tested my patience, but eventually, both men hauled in snook that stretched past forty inches.

Around mid-morning, I was eavesdropping on my clients having a conversation, and should have told them jeans, in June, on a boat, not exactly smart. Once I overheard their political subject, I zoned out and mused on the previous night, in particular on how humility can cause not just anger, but motivation to find normalcy and peace.

The phrase, "How could I be so stupid?" repeated in my head for the rest of the two-hour charter. The clients appeared to be satisfied, unaware of my inner emotional frenzy. I'd succeeded, at their request, in supplying them with the normal sand flat's troupe of characters: snook, redfish, trout, ladyfish—they had all made generous appearances.

Approaching mid-day, above, the once-pleasant white fluffs had bloomed a dark anvil cloud, tipping overhead, so we headed for the trivial safety of Ponce de Leon Park—about a thirty-minute ride. As we entered the first channel marker, growling thunder echoed above, and the first raindrop fell and hit the white front deck of my skiff. The two men were debating over who had caught the largest snook, paying no attention to the gathering moisture.

A red truck parked at the Peace River Wildlife Center caught my attention. It was the red Colorado.

I smiled.

After a few moments of recap, I informed the men that I had to get moving if I wanted to stay semi-dry. The two men thanked me for showing up and rushed for the cover of their vehicle. I didn't waste time making way from the deep sailboat channel and forced the skiff on plane before reaching the end of marker row. Cutting south, I raised the jack plate. Now running the skiff skinny, I hugged the mangroves, rounding Whore House Point. Now passing Poacher's Cut, a barrier of rain chased me along the eastern wall of Charlotte Harbor like a game of tag. As if teasing me, clouds began to release marble-sized raindrops that dripped from the bill of my visor. Mother Nature's own way of reminding me of who ran the show.

I was soaked as I coasted into my home port. The hard downpour hit the placidity of the lake like a boiling pot of water.

I idled to the dock, rounding the small sandy shoal, which Scupper, as of late, found useful as an island refuge. I passed Flip's quaint residence with a smile. He had returned.

Inside my house, the smell of panting dog was overwhelming. I readied Scupper and let her loose. She jetted through the screened lanai door, head down, nose leading her to the perfect spot to take care of business.

Spiky rain hammered the roof while I liberated from the wet clothes clinging to my body. After I found a towel, I managed a poor man's shower. Rainwater wasn't ideal for cleaning a human, but for now it would do. Next, I snagged a warm beer from the cooler and sat on the lanai, overlooking the hundreds of feet of backyard. Only the top of the houseboat was visible.

The rain finished, and after doing chores, including cleaning the skiff, I reached for my phone, scrolled to the previous call list, and sent a text to Sara.

Dinner?

Where? The smile on my face was attributed to her quick reply.

Here?

Okay, I'll stop and grab Chinese?

Perfect!

See you soon.

I reached for the scratch paper with Grahams's number and dialed. As it rang, I walked to the lanai window and glanced out at the setting sun. After two rings, he picked up.

"Captain?" Graham asked. He'd been expecting my call. This was the first time I'd used my personal cell to call him. Then, *Tyler*, I thought.

"Indeed, it is," I replied after a five-second pause.

He sensed my defeat. "Are you surprised?"

I sighed. "I'm not going to lie ... more like humiliated. It's kind of unfair that you were going to give the money to Pete the whole time but decided on leading me to believe otherwise."

"You're right in that respect, and for that I apologize. It was very noble of you to do what you did ... or try."

I replied asking the one question I'd been confused about most. "Why didn't you just tell me about Pete at the warehouse?"

"My intentions were to tell you, and I believe I attempted to do so. But you kept cutting me off, and after the rude accusations regarding empathy, I decided on a different route. So, I decided to share the money with you. I don't like losing, you see? I didn't want you to find out the way you did. I honestly thought, and hoped, you'd take the money right from the get-go—not dilly-dally around for a day. But again, I attempted to tell you multiple times, but part of me has little patience to let someone tell me what I need to do. I'm sure you can understand that."

It wasn't the answer I wanted but I didn't want to press, said, "I'm not calling you to tell you we have a deal. I'm calling you to tell you we *don't* have a deal." It was the last move I could make to regain my dignity.

"I … I don't understand?"

"I don't want your money. None of it."

"You don't?" he asked—then added, "I'm sorry to hear that. I was counting on Tyler being capable enough to show you … the bigger picture."

"Don't worry," I told him. "I'll destroy the video, and you don't have to worry about me keeping my word. It *will* be gone."

"How can I be sure?"

"You'll just have to trust me."

His tone hardened. "I'm sure by now you're aware that isn't how I do business."

"I'm not sure if *you're* aware or not, but I'd like this to be over just as soon as you."

"Oh, I doubt that," he said and breathed deep, exhaling into the mic. "I don't like being toyed with, Captain."

"This is no toy," I told him. "I'm no rat, and my word is more valuable than a solid gold mullet."

"After the events of the past couple days, and your persistence to your cause, at this point, I have no reason not to believe you, so, I guess we'll see, won't we?"

I shrug off the idle threat. "I would like to know one thing, though?"

"And what would that be?"

"Your business partner, Carl ... he was the polygraph examiner, wasn't he?"

"He was, yes," the man answered.

"That's how they were able to fool the tournament official?"

"Yes," he answered, and took a long nasally breath and relaxed. "Well, not exactly ... the polygraph test wasn't rigged. Brant and Tyler did pass it, which was a surprise to Carl at the time. He did no such tampering. Carl was in place as a precautionary measure."

"How did they pass it?" I let it soak in for a minute, lending the old man time to think. I finished with, "The tournament official was in the tent too, so they must have had some help."

"I'm not sure what you're getting at, Captain," he replied. "From what I'm aware of, they had no help what so-ever."

I was almost positive that the *Propranolol* I found in the bathroom at the party was the slight edge that the two cheaters needed to come away from polygraph cleaner than a picked dry oyster. *Propranolol* causes a slight dip in blood pressure and heart rate and eases nervousness. Surgeons were known to use it to steady their hands during stressful surgeries. I didn't press the fact that I thought they had some prescription help. It was over. I saw no need to accuse Brant of stealing his dad's pills.

"I understand," I replied, but wanted off this call, so rushed to end our conversation. "Well, if we meet again, I hope it's under different circumstances."

"Keep my number," he replied. "If you're ever in need of any kind of … let's say advantage … give me a call."

The nerve. I could sense his shit-eating grin through the phone, so I rudely replied, "Will do," and hung up.

I swigged the last sip of beer and drank another. I held my phone, flipped through the videos, found the one starring Brant and Tyler, and pressed play.

A man on video, now identified as Tyler Christianson, leaned over the bow of the Pathfinder, and using a boat hook, snagged the rope attached to the trap. A blue, fifty-five-gallon drum was then lifted and pinned against the freeboard to let the water drain. Grass, sand, and muck emitted from quarter-sized holes that had been drilled across the entirety of its blue shell.

Brant, in the tower, controlling the boat via thrust and draw, kept steady for Tyler as the tea-color water strained from the drum. Tyler then proceeded to lift each redfish after manhandling them from the trap. He presented each to Brant—an approval was necessary. The last ones were culled into the live well. I had seen enough.

I pressed delete. "Gone," I said out loud, and sent a text to both Cliff and Klinger to do the same.

I let Scupper inside, put on Bob Dylan, and had a nice moment in the chair. Scupper sat beside me—felt her forehead muscles under my hand, tail flat on the floor, sweeping back and forth, eyes fixed on mine.

Suddenly, there was a knock at the door.

I staggered, not expecting Sara so soon, but the person behind the door wasn't Sara. It was Dr. Clara. I took a deep breath, then stepped back. "What is she doing here?"

"Just a minute," I told her, and leaped into the spare bathroom and glanced at the mirror, checking my hygiene. Even after the rain shower, the slight stench of sweat and sunscreen still lingered. After a sniff test, I realized that this wasn't the best I'd ever smelled. "I don't need to impress her," I mumbled.

I shook off the surprised nervousness, lost the towel, put on a pair of board shorts, and opened the door.

"Clara … what brings you—?"

She stomped through the door, uninvited. I plodded aside, then peeked into the street. Sara was on her way.

Her rant began contentiously. "Well, Shamus, I've got to hand it to you. You sure haven't changed."

"Didn't know I was supposed to…"

"Really?" She stood straight, a mature, demanding pose.

"I don't know what you're talking about, really."

"Oh, don't play coy, Shamus. You know *exactly* what I'm talking about."

I made one last attempt to conceal my knowledge. "Clara, I've really got no idea what you're getting at."

As though she owned the place, she continued straight through to the kitchen, dropping her brick-like purse onto the wooden kitchen table. Her eyes were wide, had bags, somewhat strung-out. "How did you find out?" she asked. She was wearing the usual blue scrubs, sneakers, hair tied up in a bun and red, bold framed glasses resting halfway down her nose.

"Find out about what?"

"The tournament."

"The tournament?" I asked, feeling the pressure. "The one this weekend? Everyone knows about that. It's very popular—"

She cut me off. "How *long* do you want to go around in circles like this? Because I'll go *allll* day." Now her hand rested on her hips.

Sensing Sara's arrival, I decided to cave: "Oh, you mean the one this weekend that your boyfriend cheated on?"

"That's the one," she answered. "Why did you have to stick your nose in this?" Her voice rose. "Can't let one go?"

"Wait, how did you know about that anyway?"

"I'm dating Brant, remember?"

"Did he tell you he cheated? Him, and his buddy, Tyler?"

"No, he didn't. I put two and two together and figured it out *all* by myself."

I laughed at her problem-solving skills. "You're a vet, not Sherlock Holmes."

Her demeanor toughened and her eyes closed. Air pulled in through her nose. I always thought she was the most beautiful when she was upset. Maybe I pissed her off on purpose, just to see that beauty again.

"Anyway," she said, "...things were going *just* fine—Brant and I—then you had to come along and mess everything up. You and your honesty and integrity, always doing the right thing. Well, this time you went *too* far."

"Okay … I'm missing something, I think."

"Shamus, Brant was lying to me the whole time. He said that he wasn't cheating, even after I questioned him over and over. He said that he and Tyler won honestly, but I knew something was up. They went out on the boat the night before and then early after the tournament. They said they were pre-fishing, but I saw the barrels! And after I saw you at Hooters, I got suspicious. Brant was acting weird when he returned to the table."

"You know why they cheated in the first place right?" I suddenly felt like the devil's advocate.

"Yes, I know *now*, but he lied to me! If he had just told me from the beginning, then it wouldn't have been a big deal, but…"

For some reason I felt her pain. "I'm trying to figure out why you're making a big deal about this. I mean, the guy cheated to give money to a man on his last breath. You can't be *that* mad at him."

"Trust me, I'm not mad about that," she replied. "I'm mad that he didn't trust me enough to let me in on what was *really* going on."

I muttered, "Women and their trust…"

"What?"

"Nothing, nothing," I replied. "I'm just trying to explain that I think you're making a big deal out of this. I'm sure he had his reasons to cheat."

Her head was down, picking at a hangnail. "Maybe, but—"

"If you don't mind me asking, what do you see in him anyway? He's kind of a doofus."

Her eyes flipped up, slanted. "What does *that* mean?"

I stepped toward the window overlooking the backyard. "I think you can do much better, that's all."

Her eyes opened wide. "What? Like you?"

"No, not like me."

She thought for a silent moment. "I don't know. He's simple."

"Simple? That's it?"

"Yeah, simple. Not complicated, *like you*."

"Me? Complicated? That makes *no* sense."

"I'm just saying you have things that you're passionate about. Things that you stand up for," she explained, but then corrected, "I meant to say *depth*. You have much more depth, and Brant, well, not so much."

I took the comment for what it was. "Okay, if you say so. If I remembered correctly, you weren't so fond of those depths when *we* were dating."

She stepped closer, sliding her finger overtop the polyurethane-stained wooden table, as if checking for dust. She moved a step closer, though her legs didn't move, just hips. "Why did I let you go, Shamus?"

Her words shifted everything, sharp as a lightning strike. I felt her wanting me—subtle, wordless, and impossible to ignore. I realized the dangers of letting them in and blocked. "If I remember correctly, it was you who decided that *we* wanted different things, remember?"

She stopped in mid-stride and squinted as though I'd ruined the party. "So, where is the pup?" She swiveled toward the lanai.

"Oh, she's outside running amok. She's made an unlikely friendship out back with the resident dolphin."

Now, seemingly in a playful mood, she balanced on one leg. "Fun fact: Dolphins don't actually sleep.

They're always sleeping and always awake at the same time. One half of their brain sleeps while the other stays awake. Cool, huh?" One thing I missed about Clara was her fun animal facts.

"I did-not-know that."

She saw me glance at my watch. "Am I keeping you from something? Or someone…?"

"I am expecting company any minute, yes."

"Your *girlfriend*?"

"You could say that, yes." It felt good to say it.

She stared in my eyes, pressing to seduce, probing for glimpses of doubt, so to advance her campaign. Her eyes were brown like acorns; scrubs flattering a magnificent body underneath. I looked away.

Next, I did something that I would regret for a long, long time. I stepped back. "I don't think we should do this. I'm sorry."

She pouted up her lip. "What are you? In *love* with her?"

"I'm not sure that's any of your business, but, really, it's getting late." I led her toward the door.

She stopped mid-step. "Oh, I forgot." She reached into her purse and pulled out an envelope and handed it to me.

"What's this?"

"Scupper's bill."

She slid past me while I opened the door and I caught the scent of vet office as she crossed the threshold. It took one deep breath to take it all in.

She didn't wave after I saw her out, but swung around the large purse, stepping to the driveway, and then lifted into a Jeep. My chest expanded like re-inflating an airless innertube. I breathed again as her tires kicked up dust while she sped off. "Did I just do the right thing?" I said to myself. "That was a side of Clara I had *not* seen in a *long* time. Brant's mistrust has brought her scandalous side to the surface—impressive *and* intriguing."

I left the front entry open and closed the screen door to block the mosquitoes. Clara's scent still lingered, so I found a match, struck it, and returned to the lanai.

****

Rain had moved on, leaving the clouds ragged and thin, offering the lingering light one final chance to spread across the sky. The basin's black surface mirrored the red sun above as it dipped to the horizon. A school of mullet leap-frogged through the air. Spinner, underneath, had schooled them tight, biting one in her mouth like a dog with a bone. Other mullet darted off for the shallowness of the oyster bed, hopeful for the safety it would provide.

I slipped on flip-flops and headed down the path to the dock, but not before grabbing another beer from the cooler. At the dock, I hopped onto the houseboat, each step sending out a small ripple. I brought the beer and two folding beach chairs up to the houseboat's top deck

No doubt the view was what had sold me the house. Sunsets have taken on a whole new meaning while sitting atop the houseboat—something about being up high, peering overtop the short mangrove wall lining the basin, granted my mind time to heal in a profound way. On a clear night sitting atop the houseboat, dozens of constellations littered the night sky. The significance of a simple sunset seemed overshadowed by the lack of existentialism left in the world. Too many distractions from what really matters.

Out ahead, Scupper stood atop the sandy shoal at the entrance to the basin, again barking at Spinner while the dolphin now circled. With Spinner nearby, I felt at ease about Scupper's swimming habit. There was nothing in the dolphin's behavior that suggested danger. But would she swim in the canal if Spinner weren't there?

Reflecting, would I've have taken Scupper to the vet if Dr. Clara wasn't there? I don't think I would've even thought about it. Visiting Dr. Clara at the vet might have been irrational, a subconscious "look at me now" kind of thing. Maybe showing off Scupper was my pathetic attempt to show her that I was indeed capable of commitment. Perhaps I'd wanted the pup for no reason other than to lead it, deliberately, to Dr. Clara office.

One thing was for sure: I acted the way I did with Graham and Brant because I believed they were cheating, and they were. In the end, the facts spoke clearly—I'd been beaten. My claims, however justified, led nowhere. The cheating was real, but I couldn't strike back. I was by-catch, tangled in a plan far more seasoned than I was. Graham knew the game. I was still learning the rules. Thirty years old might be the new twenty when it comes to experience. I had them in my net, like trapped pinfish, but in the end, they weren't the right guys. They weren't the right ones to which justice could benefit. They had to be released.

I thought back to a few days ago, on the houseboat, and wondered if Cliff hadn't needed help working the catering job, would I have been better off? Could I have saved myself from the humiliation? The answer was: I'll never know. The past is the past, and nothing is going to change it.

I was freed from thoughts when a distant screen door slapped. Sara stood a short step from the backyard doorway, a hand blocking the setting sun.

"Shamus?" she called.

I stood and waved.

She saw me, headed back in, and reappeared carrying a brown paper bag. The remaining sun shone upon a black sports bra and thin, blue yoga shorts. Her shoulder-length blonde hair swayed, and the snapping of her flip-flops reached my ears.

She held up the bag as if it were a lipped bass. I told her to hurry if she wanted to see the sunset. With long, tan legs, she treaded along the plank, crossing it like a balance beam, then stretched across to the houseboat with a small leap. I peered down at her charming face.

She said, "Hope you fancy sweet and sour chicken." Her eyes were concentrating on the ladder steps.

"You know I do." I attempted to climb down, but she stopped me.

"I've got it … just take the food, okay?" She handed over the bundle of steaming food, with two cold beers perched on top nearly sweating through the bag.

As she reached the last step, I whisked her up and into my arms—then set her down on the tops of my now bare feet.

She felt my intense hug. "Well, hello to you too, Mr. Pickford."

I released her and we both sat and unboxed our meals.

She handed me a beer from the bag, then she bit first into the chicken. "This is so good." To catch any falling pieces of food, she cupped a hand under her chin. "You wanna try it?"

I didn't answer immediately but continued observing her softly chew.

"Why don't you take a picture? It'll last longer."

"I just might."

I snatched the fork, spiked a chunk from the box of chicken, and bit. "You were right, you know…"

"Right?" she asked and then smiled. "Duh—about what?"

"Funny, but really … about how I don't let things go."

She set the chicken down and picked up a beer. "I didn't mean it in a bad way, and it's just sometimes you get ahead of yourself."

"This time I *sure* did."

"Really? What did you do *now*?"

After explaining the entire story, she told me, "If you need the satisfaction of resolution, then nothing should stand in your way … there is no shame in humility, Shamus."

I did appreciate the attempt at ego re-nourishment, but I would no doubt be mending this one solo, and over time.

Sara finished her meal, sat back in the folding chair, and stretched out her lengthy tanned legs. "Beautiful sunset from up here."

"Yeah," I replied, gaze turning toward her— adding, "Hopefully many more to come."

Sara squinted, used her hand as a visor. Something caught her attention as the last blip of sun dipped below the horizon. "Is that Scuppers?"

"Oh—yeah," I glanced. "She's out playing … with Spinner."

She slapped my knee. "Shamus!"

"What?" I answered.

"Shamus, she's gonna drown you keep lettin' her swim out there!"

In a calming voice, I told her, "I think she'll be *just* fine."

After hearing Sara's voice, Scupper was now doing the ol' doggie paddle, heading toward the ramp. A few minutes later Sara leaned over the ledge and watched the pup swim.

Scupper trotted sluggishly the first few steps onto the boat ramp, paused, and shook herself dry. I called her to the houseboat, and she rounded a small sable palm at full bore, igniting some sort of enthusiasm reserve tank. She hit the plank and slowed to a careful trot. Her tail wagged as she found my face. Sara leaned over the edge and observed Scupper in disbelief. "Is that what I think it is?"

"Depends on what you think it is…"

"You put her in a pet life jacket?"

"Sure did, and she loves it. Hates when I take it off."

She paused, face formed to an endearing expression, and then threw herself on top, knocking me over. "*What* am I going to do with you?"

"You can start by kissing me."

The End

You can contact David Earth here:
earthtodavid101@gmail.com

If you leave a supporting review, it would be much appreciated.